You are cordially invited to...

Honor *thy pledge*

to the

Miami Confidential Agency

Do you hereby swear to uphold
the law to the best of your ability...

To maintain the level of integrity of this
agency by your compassion for victims,
loyalty to your brothers and sisters and
courage under fire...

To hold all information and identities
in the strictest confidence...

Or die before breaking the code?

DANA MARTON

BRIDAL OP

HARLEQUIN®

TORONTO • NEW YORK • LONDON
AMSTERDAM • PARIS • SYDNEY • HAMBURG
STOCKHOLM • ATHENS • TOKYO • MILAN • MADRID
PRAGUE • WARSAW • BUDAPEST • AUCKLAND

ACKNOWLEDGMENT:
Special thanks and acknowledgment are given to Dana Marton
for her contribution to the MIAMI CONFIDENTIAL miniseries.

I would like to dedicate this book to my friend Maggie Scillia.
Thank you for all your help and support! I would also like to thank my
wonderful editor, Allison Lyons, and the fabulous writers I was lucky to
be working with on Miami Confidential: B.J. Daniels, Kelsey Roberts
and Mallory Kane. My most sincere appreciation to Tracy Montoya, one
of my favorite writers, for helping me with those Spanish expressions.

ISBN-13: 978-0-373-88707-1
ISBN-10:   0-373-88707-8

BRIDAL OP

Copyright: © 2006 by Harlequin Books S.A.

www.eHarlequin.com

Printed in U.S.A.

ABOUT THE AUTHOR

Author Dana Marton lives near Wilmington, Delaware. She has been an avid reader since childhood and has a master's degree in writing popular fiction. When not writing, she can be found either in her garden or her home library. For more information on the author and her other novels, please visit her Web site at www.danamarton.com.

She would love to hear from her readers via e-mail: DanaMarton@yahoo.com.

Books by Dana Marton

HARLEQUIN INTRIGUE
806—SHADOW SOLDIER
821—SECRET SOLDIER
859—THE SHEIK'S SAFETY
875—CAMOUFLAGE HEART
902—ROGUE SOLDIER
917—PROTECTIVE MEASURES
933—BRIDAL OP

CAST OF CHARACTERS

Isabelle Rush—Miami Confidential agent and spokeswoman for Weddings Your Way. Used to doing things on her own terms, Isabelle refuses to let a man tell her what to do or how to do it. Including Rafe.

Rafe Montoya—A former DEA agent who is now working for Miami Confidential. He's admired Isabelle Rush as a coworker, but now that they're on a mission together, can he handle the sparks they're igniting?

Sonya Botero—A society belle about to be married to Juan DeLeon. She was kidnapped in front of Weddings Your Way.

Juan DeLeon—Sonya's fiancé wields considerable political power in Ladera, which earned him a number of enemies.

Maggie DeLeon—Juan's ex-wife lives in an insane asylum. Is she as broken as she seems, or is she living for revenge?

Alberto Martinez—A political opponent of Juan DeLeon who would like nothing more than to see Juan crushed. But how far would he go to distract Juan from politics?

Prologue

Miami, U.S.A.
June 20, 2006

Jose Fuentes waited in the back of the vintage limousine for his victim and watched the street, aware of a number of things at once: the expensively dressed man and woman exiting Weddings Your Way—looking less than happy—the few cars passing by, the comfort of the spacious backseat beneath him. His fingers fluttered over the black leather in a soft caress. Maybe when this was all over he would get his own limo. Or maybe not. Better not draw attention to his person or his wealth.

And when he was done with Botero, he *would* be wealthy.

Sunshine reflected off the pavement and the white walls of exclusive villas; palm trees swayed in the breeze coming off the bay. His window down a crack, he could smell the water. He liked Miami. Someday, he might come back here on vacation.

His phone chirped. Annoyance replaced his pleasant mood as he recognized the number.

Good work took time.

"Patience," he said as he picked up the call.

"You don't have her yet?" The voice was full of censure.

"She's a few minutes late." He pulled the cell phone from his ear to glance at the exact time displayed on its small LCD screen and caught sight of the white limo he'd been waiting for as it turned the corner.

Time to get the ball rolling.

"I'll call you back." He clicked off and nodded to Gordy behind the wheel, a man he trusted but would take care of afterward nevertheless. Gordy had a number of useful attributes, but the ability to rise above his circumstances wasn't one of them. No matter how big a share of the money he would get, sooner or later he would find his way back to the booze and the drugs and the old friends he could get them from.

And then Gordy would talk.

That worried him, how the number of people involved was snowballing out of control. Why was Ramon in Miami, for example? To supervise him? The thought that he wouldn't be trusted filled him with rage. Not that he trusted any of the men on either crew, the one he'd brought to Miami or the one he'd put together to stay in Ladera to wait for Sonya there, under Pedro Carrera's direction. Pedro was going to be pissed after he figured out he'd been screwed over, stuck with a high-profile kidnap victim on his hands.

Jose shrugged off the thought. Carrera could be as pissed as he wanted to be as long as the man didn't find him. And, with as much money as he was going to make on this deal, disappearing without a trace shouldn't be too hard.

He glanced at the two men in the back of the limo with him. They were there for muscle—a kidnapping in broad daylight in the middle of Miami took more than one pair of hands. He wasn't about to show himself. He was going to play this smart, planned and coordinated. This was his chance to break out, to leave small-time and give himself a promotion.

Once they had Sonya, these two would smuggle her out of the country, to Pedro in Ladera. Jose and the rest of the team would stay behind to tie up loose ends. He would pick up the ransom money and ditch the master plan at that point, start following his own path. He wasn't going back to Ladera. Ever. He was going in the opposite direction. And when he got there, he'd buy himself the life he deserved.

"Get ready," he said to the men as Sonya Botero's sleek new limo pulled up to the curb.

Johnson, her driver, got out and opened the door for her. The rich bitch who'd exited the bridal salon a few minutes ago stopped to watch. What was she doing? Hoping to spot a celebrity?

Well, hell, he didn't have time to worry about her.

"Watch for the security cameras. You know where they are," he said.

Gordy pulled the car up behind Botero's; his other two men jumped from the car and dashed for Sonya as planned.

What the hell was her driver doing? Why was he putting up a fight?

Okay, not much of a fight, just enough to make it look good. Stupid bastard still thought he'd do his part and get out with his pay. He'd be taken care of before the day was out.

Then Sonya was in the car, on the seat opposite from him, and the doors slammed shut.

"Who are you? What do you want? Why are you doing this to me?" She started on a tone of outrage but finished the last sentence on a sob, her eyes wide with panic. "Please—" She yanked her head around as a needle sank into her arm—along with a drug, courtesy of Dr. Ramon, the man proving useful for something after all. She tried to jerk away but was held firmly until she gave up struggling.

Gordy put the car in Reverse.

Botero's driver was still on the ground, playing his role to the hilt.

Jose Fuentes considered him for a second. Might as well take care of him now. No sense letting the police have a go at him. "Run the bastard over."

Gordy complied, but Johnson rolled out of the way.

The man who'd been there with his ritzy bimbo since before Sonya's arrival was rushing toward them, looking hell-bent on playing saviour.

What the hell did he think he had to do with any of this? Had a hero complex, did he? Anybody that stupid didn't deserve to live. "Get the bastard."

Gordy turned the steering wheel and aimed toward the man, but he dove aside. Had pretty good reflexes, that one. The woman, standing a few yards behind him, wasn't as nimble. She took the full brunt of the hit, bouncing off the hood with a satisfying thud.

One less witness. Jose clicked his tongue with satisfaction that was short-lived.

People were running from up the street and Weddings Your Way. He didn't like the look of one in particular, a tall Hispanic guy who was pulling a small handgun as he ran. Probably their in-house security. Seemed like nobody could mind their own damned business.

"Go! Go! Go!"

Gordy aimed the limo into the city, toward the dark garage that was ready with another car to make the switch. Like clockwork, that's how it would all go. The initial idea might not have been his, but by God he'd done the on-site planning. Their success would be due to him and no one else.

Gordy flew through the red light at the intersection, dodging cars like a pro, proving he was the right man for the job. A minute later they were lost in traffic, just a few blocks from being safe.

Jose Fuentes picked up the phone, ready to report now. Had to keep everyone happy and make sure nobody suspected a thing until after he'd gone his own way.

He bit back a smile as he dialed. The first part of his mission had been accomplished. He was eager to move on to the next phase.

Chapter One

A few weeks later

She shouldn't have agreed to the mission.

Isabelle Rush hung on to the rock ledge with the tip of her fingers, dangling over a 300-foot drop to the rocks below. A tangy scent from some small fern she'd inadvertently crushed in the last handhold tickled her nose. Would she fall if she sneezed?

She was secured with knots and ropes she didn't understand and didn't trust, petrified of slipping. The current of air that moved above the tree line seemed to pick up speed, the odd gusts pushing against her.

Please, don't let there be a serious wind.

"A few more yards and we can stop to

rest," Rafe said from somewhere above her, barely breathing heavily.

She, on the other hand, was gasping for oxygen in the thin, high-altitude air, sweat running down her back from exertion.

She should have stayed in Miami.

He was the absolute worst man for her to be teamed up with. Of course she couldn't refuse, not when a client's life hung in the balance.

But, at the very least, when Rafe had said "shortcut" she should have run screaming into the night—in the opposite direction. What was it with men and their shortcuts? Like chasing murderous, kidnapping drug lords wasn't enough excitement? They had to add getting lost in the Andes Mountains to the mix?

"This will save us a full extra day," he said as he tightened the rope.

She hoped he was right and that her instincts, which screamed *lost* and *on the brink of disaster,* were sounding a false alarm. Speed was their only hope for finding Sonya Botero alive.

Isabelle clenched her muscles, having a foothold for one boot only and too much of a gap between the next indentation to push or pull herself up. She was five foot four. She could not stretch over the same distance as Rafe could.

Night was closing in on them—not dark yet, but the shadows were becoming long, which made judging distances harder. She had to do something before visibility became worse and her limbs grew even more exhausted. *One... Two...* She heaved her body upward, looking at the chunk of rock she was aiming for, shutting out the drop below. She grabbed on, and in that moment of truth that decided whether she would hold her grip or fall, a strong hand clamped around her wrist and held her steady.

"Easy now," Rafe said. "Almost there."

She allowed him to pull her up, only grunting in response although she had plenty to say. She was saving her breath for the climb. Rafe, having been born in Ladera, seemed used to the mountains that made up most of the country.

He helped her up to a ledge that was about six feet by four feet, small patches of moss growing in the scant dirt the winds had blown up there. The rock wall continued above it for another hundred feet at least, just as sheer as the section they'd already conquered.

"Nice climb." A sense of relief was evident in his smile, the fact that he was immensely enjoying himself visible in his eyes—the color of cocoa powder the instant it melts into chocolate. "Piece of cake, didn't I tell you?" His voice was rich with the flavor of South America, spiced with the slightest accent.

"Mmm." She gulped the thin air. When he'd pulled her up she'd landed on her knees. She sat back onto her heels now and shrugged off her backpack, blew on her fingertips, which were raw and bruised from the sharp rocks they'd had to conquer.

"How is this better than taking a car up the road?" she asked, once she thought she could speak without gasping.

"Faster," he said over his shoulder as he unhooked their ropes systematically. "I'm glad we picked the Maxim ropes—excellent hand, 48-sheath yarn, good twist level." He was gathering up everything in careful coils. "Fine abrasion resistance, too. See this? Not a worn spot."

Was that supposed to make sense? "So

how come you've never mentioned anything about this climbing hobby of yours?"

He shrugged and tucked the equipment against the inside edge of the shelter. "Never came up, I guess."

She didn't mean to voice the thought that popped into her head, but it came out just the same. "We've worked together for three years and I barely know anything about you."

Part of that was his own need for privacy, she supposed, and part that she had, on purpose, kept out of his way, not liking the physical attraction that drew her to a colleague, an infamous playboy at that. A brief and steamy relationship that would no doubt end in pain and embarrassment was not among her carefully crafted life goals.

He was unrolling his sleeping bag, saying something about the time they would save by climbing.

"Faster is not always better," she snapped. Not if one of them got injured or fell.

"No, not in everything."

When he looked at her like that, his full attention like a cocoon around her, his brown eyes fixed on her face, it made her want to squirm like some schoolgirl. She gathered her self-control and kept her poise as he went on.

"The road is probably watched. It's not a bad climb, honestly. Just seems like it because it's your first. We have good equipment. I'm not going to let anything happen to you."

"Last I checked, we were here as teammates," she said, testy that he made it sound as if he was babysitting her.

"Of course. And I hope you are not going to let anything happen to me." His sensuous lips stretched into a smile, his even white teeth a contrast to his olive-colored skin. "*Compadres.* Buddies."

That'll happen. Partners, yes. Buddies, highly unlikely. She wasn't optimistic enough to shoot for friendship. She wasn't sure she could handle it, didn't want to spend that much time with him outside the job. The forced proximity of the mission was plenty enough to drive her crazy.

None of that was his fault, though, to be fair. "Sorry," she said. "I'm just tired. It's been a nerve-racking day."

"Are you hurt anywhere?" he asked as he came closer.

She pulled her hands to her lap, but he caught the gesture and reached for them, took one in each of his and flipped them palm up.

His face turned grim as he swore softly under his breath in Spanish. He let her left hand go and reached for his backpack to extract a small tube of ointment from one of the side packets. "Why didn't you say something? We could have taken more breaks."

"Call me crazy, but I don't consider dangling on a rope over the abyss a break. I'd just as soon get the climb over with as fast as possible." She took a breath then held it as he squeezed some of the clear gel onto his fingertip and rubbed it gently over the pad of her thumb.

"Okay?" He glanced up, into her eyes, with concern.

She cleared her throat. "Good. Feels cool."

"You should be fine by morning." He moved on to the next finger, then the next.

When he was done, he took her hands one more time and pressed a warm kiss into each palm, sending some heat into her face that she hoped he couldn't see in the twilight.

"How are your arms and legs?" He put

away the gel. "A good muscle rub and everything could be as good as new by the time we get going again."

"No. Thanks," she said and fished out a jar of face cream from the bottom of her pack, something one of her friends was developing in a quest to build a successful cosmetics business.

Isabelle got free samples of everything, partially due to their friendship and partially, she suspected, because Sylvia was hoping to feature her products, for future brides, at Weddings Your Way. She dabbed the smooth, rich cream onto her wind-dried face with a knuckle and spread it around with the back of her hand, not wanting to mess up whatever potion Rafe had rubbed over her fingertips.

The scent of oranges soothed her. Sylvia used various essential oils in most everything she made.

Rafe sniffed the air appreciatively. "So we snuggle up for the night?" He flashed a sly grin and made himself comfortable.

"No. Again. But nice try," she said while thinking a snuggle wouldn't be that bad, for body heat if nothing else. August was a winter month in Ladera, a country in the Southern hemisphere. The weather wasn't bad during the day but dipped into the forties at night. At least Laderan winters were generally dry, so they didn't have to worry about being cold *and* wet.

The breeze ruffled his dark hair, putting the slight curls into disarray. "Men have fragile egos, you know," he said, and his expression turned serious. "Too much rejection can be psychologically damaging. Emotional trauma and that kind of stuff."

She drew up an eyebrow. "I don't think you see enough rejection for that."

He was unfairly good looking, something like she pictured Antonio Banderas would look like if he joined a gym today and kept going religiously. He had an easy smile, sexy, that matched his laid-back manner, and intense eyes that were sharp with intelligence. He was infinitely charming and, at the same time, commanded respect with ease.

And she was a fool for getting a secret thrill out of bantering with him like this, although she was smart enough never to take his advances seriously—nor did she think he expected her to.

The man had an active social life. She always figured he flirted with her at the office out of boredom in between assignments.

"Someday..." he said, mischief glinting in his eyes, obviously not ready to give up yet "...all that pent-up desire will erupt. You will realize what you've been missing. The dam will break and—"

"Is this little fantasy going anywhere?" she asked in a voice as dry as she could manage it.

"I'm just saying. When the time comes... Be gentle with me."

She smiled into the semidarkness despite herself. "I'm not someone you need to worry about."

"It's always the quiet ones who worry me the most."

His voice vibrated through her the way bass chords did if you sat too close to the speakers.

Don't think about it.

She half turned and dug through her backpack for food and water. Next time she agreed to go on a mission with anyone, she was going to insist on hotel rooms—separate ones. She glanced around their cramped shelter and considered it fully for the first time. *Pitiful.*

"Should have stayed a criminologist at the Drug Enforcement Agency," she muttered.

"But isn't this more fun?" A smile hovered above his lips.

"I liked symposiums and consultations with local police. Court appearances to give expert testimony definitely beat wondering if any poisonous bugs will crawl into my sleeping bag." Or snakes. She swallowed.

She should have thought of that before she'd signed up to be an undercover agent at Miami Confidential. But she'd given up her comfortable job of profiling and in-house suspect interviews, partially because the offer from Miami Confidential had been hard to turn down and because she'd seen it as another new challenge to prove that she could stand her ground anywhere, do anything a man could. It was something her father had taught her at an early age, at times when having four brothers had overwhelmed her.

She thought of her work at the DEA then glanced around at the narrow ledge that was to be their resting place for the night. Now that she was with Miami Confidential, she had a feeling she could kiss assignments that came with room service goodbye.

"Snakes can't climb this high, can they?" she asked, to be sure.

He was playing with the phone, trying to make a connection. "What would be the point? Nothing's up here. They stay where their prey is."

Damn smart of them.

"Okay. Good." She nodded. "Anything?" she asked after a while.

He shook his head. "Even satellite phones don't work everywhere."

"We'll report back once we reach the top." She hoped and prayed they would make it that far.

"Not much left for tomorrow—an hour's worth of climbing at best. But it's tricky."

Tricky? What the hell was the wall-of-death they'd just conquered? "Worse than up to here?"

"We'll be getting to the part where the rock is covered with soil."

And soil crumbled, slipped. "Great."

"Plus we'll be above the tree line," he added. "We could be spotted."

"All this good news is overwhelming."

"We can handle it."

Damn right they would. Failure was not an option. She wasn't going to let Sonya die.

"She was still alive four days ago." She kept telling herself that throughout the day, hanging on to the thought for hope.

The last time Carlos Botero had been contacted he had demanded to hear Sonya's voice. The contact the kidnappers allowed had been brief but sufficient to reassure the father. "We have no reason to think anything has changed since then. Rachel will call us as soon as anything new comes in."

The whole case was full of oddities, starting with the ransom note. It had been delivered to Sonya's father instead of her fiancé, Juan DeLeon, a powerful politician. Why? Did that have significance or was it random choice? Both men were wealthy and powerful.

"I keep thinking there's more at stake here than money. The kidnappers have to be from Ladera. Otherwise, why bring Sonya here? It only makes sense if they know the country like the back of their hands, if they're sure they can hide out more effectively here." She paused. "But if they're Laderan, they have to be more familiar with Juan than with Botero. Why not send the note to him? Or why not kidnap Sonya in Ladera in the first place? Law enforcement is a lot more lax here. She's been spending as much time here lately as she does at home." They'd been over the same questions before. But maybe if they kept asking them, eventually one of them would come up with the correct answer.

"They want to keep the focus away from the country."

She nodded, still agreeing with the conclusion they kept coming up with every time they talked about the clues. At least, as far as they knew, the kidnapers were not aware that Miami Confidential now had Sonya's true location.

"I—" She fell silent then went ahead and, for the first time, voiced the thought she knew had been creeping around in both their heads. "I don't think they're bringing her back."

His face darkened. "No. Transporting her across borders was way too much risk the first time around. They'd have to be stupid to try that again."

"They never meant to return her." Her words hung with a heavy finality in the air between them.

He shook his head. "I don't think so. They'll keep her alive as long as they need her in case Botero asks to hear her voice. As soon as they have the money..."

He didn't have to finish.

"It's about politics," he said with conviction. "Juan has a number of bills on the table, bills that would cut in to the drug trade, bills that would alter some political processes. The House is in session. His bills are coming up for a vote soon. Someone wants him distracted and far from Ladera. They know he's not coming back from the U.S. as long as he thinks Sonya is still there. The longer he is away from home, the more time his enemies have to conspire against him and make sure his bills fail."

"Maybe," she said.

"But?"

"I don't know. Doesn't feel right to me."

"You don't think Juan is the real target? Someone tried to shoot him a few weeks before the kidnapping. Hell of a coincidence."

"Of course Juan is the target," she said, agreeing with him up to that point. "I just don't think the kidnapping is politically motivated."

"Right. Because *it doesn't feel right.*"

"I just think that the fact that whoever is trying to get to Juan DeLeon is doing it through his fiancée has some significance."

"His ex-wife, Maggie, is locked up in an insane asylum," he said, repeating an earlier argument. "Sean checked her out."

Of course, he was absolutely right, frustrating as it was. And yet, her instincts were definitely pulling her in Maggie's, the ex-wife's, direction. "The only people caught so far that we know for sure were involved with the kidnapping were Maggie's doctor, Dr. Ramon and her cousin, Jose Fuentes. The only reason we even know that Sonya is at the army base is because Fuentes confessed it before he bled out."

"He never confessed a connection to Maggie."

"He couldn't very well tell his life story, could he? He didn't live long enough, for heaven's sake."

"And if he worked for someone else?"

She considered that, determined to keep an open mind. Most of Maggie's family were well-to-do, a few of them in politics, but there were a couple of black sheep, some with ties to the drug trade. Rafe had a valid point there.

Fuentes could have worked for one of Juan's political opponents or one of his enemies in the drug trade. There were too many possibilities. His bills were making him unpopular with a lot of people.

"Anyway, the most important thing is we know where Sonya is right now," he said. "First we get her to safety, then we can figure out who was behind it all."

She nodded. If all went well, at one point tomorrow Rafe and she would see to it that Sonya Botero was freed from her captors, whomever they might work for. She hoped and prayed the woman was still alive when they got there.

"They'll keep her around for a while yet," he said, his thoughts apparently running along the same line. "For the money and because of Juan. She's just a tool to hurt him, to distract him from his political agenda. If his young, beautiful fiancée died now, think of the headlines. Think of the outpouring of sympathy he'd get, the votes. No."

She nodded. It made sense that whoever Juan's enemies were, they would go for total destruction—messing up both his career and personal life. Distract him with the kidnapping to make sure his bills fail, then finish him off by murdering the woman he loves. The plan seemed diabolically thorough. She could definitely see Maggie, year after year in the insane asylum, plotting her revenge. "The fury of a woman scorned."

"Somebody wants to go, you've got to let them. If that's how they feel, no sense in them staying, is there?" he asked. "I never understood jealousy."

"You might have to be in an actual relationship, you know, with feelings, to experience it."

"Ouch," he said, but grinned.

"Sorry." She took a deep breath. What on earth was wrong with her? When had she sunk to petty needling? Rafe Montoya's private life was none of her business. And it was certainly not her place to judge. She was an intelligent woman, she ought to be able to find a better way of dealing with her unwanted attraction toward him.

She refocused on the task at hand. "I'm concerned about how they are treating her." If they planned to kill her all along, they wouldn't worry about minor damage along the way, would they?

He nodded, sober now. He knew the criminal mind as well as she did, maybe better—from both sides of the law.

From what she'd heard when they'd worked for the DEA, he had left a rather dark past behind him when he'd moved to Miami from Ladera, although she didn't know the details. They hadn't known each other back then, worked different territories, but Rafe's busts were legendary. Then they both left the agency, he a year sooner than she had, and by chance both ended up recruited by Miami Confidential, an undercover division of the Department of Public Safety.

"How long before the vote on Juan's bills?" he asked.

"Seven days, I think." A comfortable margin. They would have Sonya out of the country long before then and safely back in Miami.

"Do you think the kidnappers will try for the money again?"

She thought for a moment. "Fuentes had shown up for it twice." And was fatally wounded by Rafe during the second handover attempt. "I'm not sure if the real mastermind who's behind all this cares that much about the money, though. If it's Juan he or she wants, then the fact that the kidnapping took place in the U.S. and that there was a ransom note to Botero—it might be all just to throw the police off the scent."

"There might not be any of the kidnappers left in Miami, except for the ones who are in custody." Two men who'd been with Fuentes had been apprehended the day he was shot. They hadn't turned out to be all that useful. Isabelle had questioned them and was fairly convinced they weren't lying when they'd claimed that they knew little of Fuentes's plan other than day-to-day instructions and had no idea whether there was a boss above Fuentes or who had Sonya in Ladera and how big the home team was here.

Her gaze strayed to the half-eaten power bar in her hand that she'd forgotten as they talked. She had packed dozens of them in preparation for the trip. She finished this one now and washed it down with a few gulps of bottled water, then lay on her back and looked up. The stars were coming out. "We better get some rest."

Rafe's backpack rustled. He was probably going for his own supper.

She stared at the night sky but could not make the feeling of endlessness and peace settle into her tense body. Was Sonya looking up at the same stars? Probably not. She'd be hidden out of sight. But her kidnappers... How many were they? She figured on a handful of men. More than that would draw attention. There might even be just one at a time. They could be guarding her in shifts.

Would they hurt her?

Her jaw tightened at the question that kept her up at night. Because she knew they might. There were a lot of things they could do to her while still keeping her in a condition good enough that, when her father demanded to hear her voice, she could say a few words over the phone.

The strong smell of spices made her glance

over at Rafe. He was chewing on some smoked meat he had bought at a local market before they'd begun their hike two days ago.

"God, I missed this." He just about moaned with pleasure.

His joy seemed so complete, she couldn't help but smile. "How long has it been since you visited?"

"Too long and not long enough." He gave her a rueful grin.

"Is there— Would you be in trouble if we ran into…" She half voiced the question that had popped into her mind from time to time since they'd landed, then stopped. She didn't want to offend him.

"Is there a warrant out for my arrest?" He drew up a black eyebrow, humor playing at the corner of his mouth. "No. Even in my most stupid younger years, I was always smart enough not to get caught." He took another bite, chewed and swallowed.

"And your old…um…associates?"

His face turned serious. "We are nowhere near them." He seemed lost in thought for a moment, then shook off whatever memories her questions had brought forth. "I'm not saying I won't be happy to be back in Miami, though."

Back to the parties, back to his women, no doubt. Oh, what did she care? "What do you tell your girlfriends when you have to leave at a moment's notice like this?" She put forward another question she'd been successfully swallowing until now.

"Family emergency," he said. "No girlfriend at the moment, if that's what you're getting at. I am conveniently available."

Her polite upbringing didn't allow her to snort or produce any other rude sound, despite the four brothers she'd grown up with—her grandmother had been a Southern belle.

As far as she could tell, Rafe was always "conveniently available" even when he did have a girlfriend, although that was a strong term for one of his temporary liaisons. Girlfriend implied commitment and some kind of semipermanence.

"Gone through the whole city already? I suppose you're going to have to move." She meant to sound humorous and winced at how bitchy her words came out.

"Very funny."

"Not really." It was sad that despite the type of man he was, she was still more attracted to him than to anyone she'd ever dated. But if they got involved and then split up, working in the same office would be murder. So she wasn't going to go there.

"I'm hoping you'll change your mind about me," he said after a while.

At thirty-four, she really was old enough to know better. "Hope is good," she said sweetly. "It's a positive emotion."

RAFE PACKED AWAY his food and lay on his back.

He would have liked to think if he really went after her, he could get her. Women had always come easy, one of the few areas of his life he never had to worry about. Isabelle, though... She was different. She was too smart by half, one of the things that attracted him to her. Probably too smart to get involved with the likes of him.

He enjoyed flirting with her at the office— gave him something to look forward to in the mornings. But he never hit on her seriously, despite that she was one of the most gorgeous women he had had the extreme good luck to meet. For one, she was a co-worker. Two, he figured she deserved someone better.

In a different world, if he were a different man… No sense in going there, no matter how many times she'd got him hot under the collar.

"We'll resume climbing at first light," he said.

"I'll be ready." She pulled a straight face, pretending hard that she wasn't petrified.

He found it fascinating to watch how she went ahead in the face of any fearsome task brought on by their mission so far. First there would be uncertainty and doubt in her eyes, then she would set those sexy lips into a firm line and seem to draw from somewhere deep within the courage necessary, pulling herself straight and unfailingly rising to the occasion.

Her sheer determination was a like a force field around her. With her normally soft, fawn-colored eyes turned hard as they were now, if she stood at the rim of their ledge, spread her arms and said that by God she was flying to the top, he would believe her.

She would conquer the rest of the cliff in the morning, he would bet his new boat on it. When the time came to climb, she would call forth the necessary strength. But for now, with a long uncomfortable night ahead of them, she looked like she could use some encouragement, a reminder of how close they were to their goal.

"If all goes well we should be at the army base by noon. We'll do some recon, pinpoint Sonya's exact location and move in as soon as it's dark again," he said, and gained heart from the thought as well.

In twenty-four hours, Sonya Botero would be safe.

She'd been nice the few times they'd met socially, long before she'd become a client at Weddings Your Way. They'd flirted once, briefly, at a party, brought together by their common Laderan heritage. Then she'd fallen for Juan DeLeon, one of Ladera's more prominent politicians. The Laderan community in Miami was all abuzz with the news.

He felt responsible for her. Not only because he'd known her before, but because, as head of security for Weddings Your Way, securing her wedding would have been his responsibility. She was kidnapped right in front of his building, under his nose. It galled him.

He hated any man who would harm a defenseless woman, use her as a pawn. He made it his personal mission to bring Sonya back and keep his partner safe in the process. Not to mention keep his hands off Isabelle. Close proximity and overpowering temptation notwithstanding.

SONYA BOTERO SHIFTED as much as her ropes let her, allowing circulation to return to her left leg, which felt as if a thousand ants were crawling all over it. She held her gaze on the leg to keep herself assured the real army of ants, the ones that had marched right through her prison hut a few days ago, had gone. She saw them now only in her repeating nightmares and would continue to see them there for a long time to come. If she lived.

Don't give up. Don't give up. Don't give up.

At least her feet had healed. She clamped on to the one positive thing she could think of. The jute sandals she'd been given at the beginning had rubbed her skin raw, and she'd been worried about developing some infection. But now that she hadn't been allowed outside for days, her wounds had had a chance to scab over and start to mend.

She thought of Juan and focused on that. Juan would come for her, Juan and her father—both men formidable in their own right.

Just a little longer. Almost over.

Trouble was, she'd been telling herself the same thing for about five weeks now, believing it a little less each day.

She couldn't give up. If she lost faith…

But faith was hard to keep when she was hurt and hungry, when her life was threatened daily. At the beginning she'd got regular meals and trips to a nearby waterfall in the evenings to clean up. Although at the time she'd thought of her captivity as unbearable, now she wished for those times back. She hadn't eaten in two days, hadn't bathed in four.

Were they growing bored with their task of guarding her? Or had something gone wrong with Miami? She'd overheard enough to know that she was being held for ransom. Where was it?

It'd be here. Soon. Juan and her father would see to it. She had to keep believing that.

Both men had lost so much already: her

father losing her twin sister to leukemia at the age of six, Juan losing his unborn son to drugs and his ex-wife to insanity. She hated the thought that now they had to worry about her.

From where she was, she could see the small fire and the men who gathered around it, drinking, one of them shoving a needle into his arm deep in the shadows. She still thought of escape now and then but no longer had the strength to attempt it.

The money is coming.
The money is coming.
The money is coming.

She repeated that over and over in her head. She knew better than to even whisper when she wasn't asked.

Chapter Two

Rafe rubbed his elbow, sore from wielding the machete all morning. "You're too close," he said, then paused. Had to be the first time he'd ever said *that* to a beautiful woman. Man, times were changing.

Isabelle dropped back.

Better. They had to keep a healthy distance between them so that if they were discovered they wouldn't both be taken out by the same spray of bullets. Drug routes crisscrossed the mountains; marijuana plantations were fairly common; poppy fields bloomed in out-of-the-way clearings. And with those came the men who guarded them, the drug lords' private armies.

Laderan army base notwithstanding, the locals knew who owned these parts and respected the real power, the men on whom their lives depended.

"What's that noise?"

Rafe stopped to listen. "Trucks. We must be getting close to the main road."

Most roads in the area were little more than footpaths that connected the mountain villages. The only paved highway for hundreds of miles led to the army base that guarded the north corner of the country. They'd been hearing planes overhead more frequently for the past few hours but couldn't see any from the thick canopy above.

He moved forward, toward the sound of the trucks, his feet sinking with every step into the layers of leaf mold underfoot. Walking on a solid surface would have been nice, but even when they found the road they would have to keep in the cover of the trees. At least he'd be able to stop navigating by his GPS unit and simply go by sight at that point.

The sound of motors faded, but he kept going forward. In another five minutes, he could see more light filter through the trees ahead. "There."

He signaled to Isabelle to keep down as they crept to the edge of the woods. Damn. He scanned the other side of the road, nothing but stumps and low brush for as far as he could see.

"Not good," he said when she came up next to him. "Loggers."

"Do we have to cross?"

"We don't have to, but I wouldn't have minded having options. I don't like it. If they're logging this far up the mountain now…"

"They might have cleared woods closer to the base, too," she finished the sentence for him.

"Right. I'd prefer not having to come out into the open." He glanced at her. She looked okay although she'd been more quiet than usual that morning—probably the side effect of the high elevation. The thin air was bothering him, too, and he'd grown up with it. "Want to stop and rest for a while?"

"Not yet. I can walk a little longer." She gave him a small smile. "I hate to stop knowing Sonya is out there, suffering who knows what." She was backing away already, a few yards into the woods where they could walk without having to worry about being seen from the road.

"If anything happens to us, Sonya is not going to be saved at all. It's okay to take a break," he reminded her. They had precious little time left, not enough for Rachel Brennan, head of Miami Confidential, or anyone else to come up with a backup plan. They had to succeed and for that they had to stay in good shape and not let themselves get too run-down.

She drew in a good lungful of air and straightened her back, visibly gathering strength. "We'll be fine." Her fawn-colored eyes glinted with determination.

"Okay," he said, just as eager to get going. "We'll eat as we go."

He moved forward, watchful and alert to any dangers ahead. They'd been lucky so far with the wildlife, but surprises abounded in the jungle. Speaking of which, the forest seemed awfully quiet all of a sudden.

He stopped again.

"What's going on?" she asked from behind him.

"Listen." He strained his ears. Was a group

of smugglers moving through the woods nearby? Maybe a predator?

He pulled his gun, Isabelle following his example.

And then he felt it, a small trembling that could easily have come from a caravan of military vehicles passing on the road, except for the lack of motor noise.

"Watch out for falling trees!" he shouted as the ground shook harder now.

She was looking at him wide-eyed, her knees bent as she tried to balance. Insects rained from the trees and she shrieked. He was over there in two leaps, covering her with his body as she crouched down.

"It's okay. Hang on. Just an earthquake." He had to continue shouting now to be heard over the groaning trees, large branches splitting and smashing to the ground around them.

Then it all stopped just as fast as it had begun.

"Just an earthquake?" she asked weakly, once the ground stopped moving.

"Happens all the time." He straightened and did his best to clean the bugs off her while she still crouched there with her shoulders hunched, apparently trying to prevent anything from crawling under her collar.

"Define *all the time,*" she said as she stood, then shivered with revulsion as she took in the ground and all the creepy crawly natives that were busy burrowing under fallen leaves or taking flight.

"A couple of hundred quakes a year. Some are so small you don't even feel them, some pretty big."

"And you haven't told me about this, because?"

"I forgot about them." He shook his head. "Isn't that weird?" There had been two big ones during his childhood. Hard to believe they'd skipped his mind. He'd been living in Miami a long time. "It's been a while."

And he'd had too many other things on his mind to remember everything he should have. He was worried about Sonya, the wildlife in the jungle, Isabelle's distracting presence and the fact that fifteen years ago, before he had left for the U.S., he had been a misguided young man, very much part of the local drug trafficking scene. If he weren't careful, he could easily run into one of

several people who'd just as soon separate
him from his skin than see him in it.

"We go this way." He picked up his
machete and struck the bundle of vines
blocking their way. "Keep behind me. Once
we reach the base, we have to get a detailed
picture of the place, find out where Sonya is,
make a plan."

He got down to business, separating a knot
of woody vines that blocked their way.

"The woods keep getting denser," she
remarked as she followed him.

"The farther north we go, the closer we
are to the equator. More vines, more bugs. A
few hundred miles ahead these woods turn
into a rain forest."

"The more you have to cut, the more notice-
able our trail is," she said between bites, eating
another one of her protein bars for lunch.

"I'm banking on the villagers and the
smugglers sticking to their own well-worn
trails. That's why we are staying off them."

They walked on for a minute or two before
she spoke again. "All right. Your turn. I'll
take the machete while you eat."

"That's not necessary." He turned around

with a *come on now* smile that quickly wilted off his face at the look in her eyes.

"So your plan is to keep up the whole *do this, don't do that, stay ten steps behind while macho man makes sure everything is okay* thing for the entire duration of this mission?" She cocked her head with a mild expression on her face.

Was she serious? "It's— I've been to the jungle before and you haven't." Her words ticked him off. "Damn right I'm going to try to protect you."

"*Protect* does not mean 'boss around,'" she said sweetly, but her eyes weren't smiling.

"You think we have enough time to hold a meeting over every little thing and discuss our differences until we come to a consensus?"

"That's not what I meant."

"Then what do you mean, exactly?"

"I meant what I said." She marched up to him. "Give me the damn machete."

She didn't look like she was kidding—her feet set apart, her gaze locked on to his face. He hated to think what this was going to do to the tender skin of her palms, which had been already damaged by the ropes. But he handed over the slightly curved blade and took a quick step back as she lifted it in an arch and went at the vegetation.

The woman used the machete like she meant it.

Maybe she was right and she needed less protection than he'd thought. He gave her plenty of room before he followed, pulling some dried meat and a bottle of water from a pocket of his backpack. He hadn't realized how hungry he was until the food hit his stomach.

They were going slower than if he was in the lead but only marginally. And being second in line wasn't a bad position after all. There were advantages—watching Isabelle twist and bend, her hair swaying around her shoulders as she went about her work with unabashed enthusiasm.

Normally, he would have regarded with caution anyone who wielded a knife that big. Oddly enough, he found the sight of her with that machete a serious turn-on. Not a surprise, come to think of it. He'd found most everything about Isabelle enticing from the moment they'd first met.

For the past few days, he had barely

thought about the fact that right now he should be out on the water, testing his brand new boat, enjoying the sunshine and the breeze instead of being sweaty and tired to the bone, trekking through the jungle. Isabelle's company more than made up for his lost vacation.

She kept up the backbreaking work for a solid hour before she slowed.

"Okay." She wiped her forehead. "You can take over for a while. Then we'll switch back."

A fine sheen of sweat dampened the strawberry-blond locks at her forehead and neck, and she was breathing hard but had a look of utter satisfaction on her face that made her irresistibly beautiful.

"Have to say, I never pictured you doing this kind of stuff—considering those high heel, strappy sandals and flirty skirts and all that you wear at the office," he teased.

"I don't wear flirty skirts," she snapped mildly, but her eyes were smiling.

"Mmm."

"Anyway, I have four brothers. I had to grow up tough," she said.

He had to admit he found this tougher,

physical side of her that was coming out in the jungle just as enticing as the soft, more cerebral role she filled at the office.

He grinned as he took the machete from her and cracked his neck before settling into the task at hand. The rest had been nice. Now that he was head of security at Weddings Your Way, his job involved a lot of desk duty, and although he made sure he kept in shape clearing brush in the jungle was a lot more strenuous than anything the trainers could throw at him at the gym.

All the more impressive that she'd done it for as long as she had.

He put some muscle into it and made progress, speaking little for the next hour or so. Then he could set the machete aside as the vegetation grew sparser again.

The sound of airplanes as they took off and landed came from fairly close by, as did other sounds of civilization—motors, metal banging against metal somewhere in the distance.

"Watch every step," he said. "I don't think the army would have perimeter sensors this far out but no sense in taking a chance."

She nodded, scanning the ground and trees around her.

They crept forward another few hundred feet before they reached the end of the woods and had to drop to their stomachs. Crawling silently, they soon reached a rocky ledge and were rewarded with an excellent overview of the small military base below.

"You think she's in there?" she whispered next to him as they lay on the rock shoulder to shoulder. "Fuentes said *at the military base.*"

"I doubt she's inside. Even if the kidnappers have connections at the base, the risk of discovery would be too great there. Can't bribe everybody." He scanned the open land and the surrounding woods. "I do think that she is someplace very close, though."

Other than the military base there were dozens of huts, a small store and other public buildings for those who made a living by selling things to the base or by working there. He could smell the pig farm before he spotted it, sprawling to the edge of the forest on the other side of the base.

"Let's circle around," he said.

"It'll go faster if we split up."

"Okay," he agreed with some reluctance. She'd proven over and over that she could handle herself. Besides, she wouldn't be part of Miami Confidential if she couldn't. "If you find anything call me on the two-way."

THAT WAS IT? He wasn't going to tell her they should stick together so he could protect her? Isabelle stared at him for a long moment, swallowing the list of objections she'd already prepared.

"All right. Good luck." She moved back toward the woods where she could circle the base without being spotted.

"Be careful," he said, and took off in the opposite direction.

She walked a good three hundred yards before she broke cover and crawled to the edge of the woods again, taking a good view at the six-foot-high cement fence and the barbed wire on top, the evenly spaced guard towers that were manned. A row of shacks had been built just outside the wall, with small kitchen gardens between them. A woman came out of one and tossed a bowl of dirty water, yelling something to the group of children who played nearby.

"*Sí, Mama,*" one of them responded.

The woman went back inside.

Isabelle counted the shacks, eleven in all. She waited and watched as more people came and went and identified the huts that nobody seemed to be using. Still, it was hard to say whether they were truly abandoned or the occupants were merely at work somewhere on the base.

A few hours remained until sunset. She couldn't go any closer than this until then, so for the time being she moved on, hoping to survey her half of the circle and meet up with Rafe somewhere ahead with a few suggestions on what they should investigate further.

The next cluster of buildings ahead was the pig farm, another two hundred yards from the huts. She pulled back into the woods where she could walk instead of having to crawl on her stomach to avoid being detected. She kept track of the distance, moving toward the base again once she thought she'd gone far enough.

She crouched for a second to listen before

she went out into the open, and the precaution paid off. Now that she wasn't moving, she could clearly make out voices, coming from the woods somewhere behind her, nearing.

She had to hide. Now.

Dense bushes edged the woods to her left. She made a dash for them and pushed inside, flattened herself to the ground. In another few minutes she could see military boots, six pairs, as men marched by toward the base.

She waited several minutes after they passed before coming out of the bushes, then another five minutes or so before moving closer to the pig farm. She breathed shallowly, her stomach turning at the stench even though plenty of open space divided the pens from the woods. Too much, in fact, to get close enough, so she had to use her binoculars to make her careful observations.

Come on. Give me something. Anything. She inspected every square foot but could see nothing out of the ordinary, nothing that aroused her suspicion.

The next stretch ahead seemed empty save an entrance gate to the base. She pulled back to the woods, planning to avoid that part altogether, not wanting to run in to soldiers. Better not to come out into the open again until she was sure she was well past the gate.

She walked carefully, knowing the woods this close to the base would hardly be deserted. The army would be training here, men hunting, older children playing.

She was right on top of the derelict hut before she could see it, so overrun by vines it was, its weather-beaten wood blending in well with its surroundings. Isabelle stopped and crouched low to the ground, took in the remains of a fire and the empty bottles a few feet from her. Every instinct in her body screamed this was it.

She circled the clearing step by careful step, stopping every few yards to listen for any sound from inside the shack. First time around, she could detect no sign of life. The second time around, she ran into Rafe.

"Any movement?" He whispered the question, his clothes a lot dirtier than when he'd left her.

She probably looked just as bad. Crawling in the dirt on your stomach tended to do that.

"Haven't seen a soul. They could be laying low," she said.

"Come up with a plan yet?"

"We wait to see how many men are in there. One of us stays here, the other could keep checking the perimeter, make sure there'll be no surprises from any side."

"Want to go?" he asked.

Putting her foot down with the machete business had apparently achieved its goal. He was taking her more seriously. Good. She liked quick learners.

But should she go? She shook her head after a moment of thought. "You have more experience in the woods."

"Okay." He pointed to the left. "If you do go anywhere, don't go near those. The thorns are full of poison."

She checked out the bushes and registered with relief that they seemed different from the ones she had thrown herself into earlier. She was definitely staying put until he got back.

By the time she returned her attention to him, he had disappeared back into the jungle. He did that well. She stared after him, unable to spot where he was.

The wind was picking up, ruffling the trees above. She couldn't detect any sound from the hut. No movement indicated the presence of men. Maybe they were sleeping. Could be they were keeping a low profile, going for the abandoned hideaway look. After the first hour went by, she began to think otherwise. The place seemed too quiet.

Was it the wrong place, after all? Was Sonya kept somewhere else?

Or had they gone off to a new hiding place? Where?

Then it occurred to her that Sonya could be in there alone, bound and gagged. Maybe they only checked on her from time to time. It would sure make the rescue easier. But even as hope fluttered through her, her instincts said it wasn't so. If they'd left her in there alone, they hadn't left her alive.

The urge to go and see for herself was overwhelming, but she stayed because it was the smart thing to do and acting stupidly now would risk not only her own life but Rafe's and the success of their mission.

She kept low and mapped the clearing in her head, the distance from the woods to the door, from the small window to the game trail on the other side.

Forty minutes passed before Rafe returned, appearing out of nowhere.

"They might all be gone," was the first thing he said, confirming her worst fears.

"Find anything?"

"Tracks. Two four-wheelers. They left sometime during the night."

She nodded and moved forward, using the vegetation for cover. They had nothing else left to do but check out the hut itself and see if they could find any clues to where the kidnappers had gone. They approached carefully, despite expecting the place to be empty. She crept toward the shabby abode while Rafe covered her, then he stole forward foot by foot while she trained her gun on the single door.

When they were both there, he opened the door a crack. Nothing happened. She pushed the door open the rest of the way with the tip of her gun.

Discarded plastic bottles littered the dirt floor, in addition to a worn-out blanket, an old wooden plate and a couple of moldy crates. The hut was small enough to be appraised with one glance.

"I doubt they're coming back." Rafe kicked the crate over, sending bugs scampering in every direction.

A shiver ran down Isabelle's back at the thought of Sonya being kept here, tied up, helpless.

"Do you think the kidnappers are taking her back to the U.S.?" Maybe they'd been wrong and Fuentes's buddies did plan on returning her in exchange for the money.

Rafe looked at her then looked away. "Wish I could be that optimistic."

He moved aside another crate, and she saw the half-dug hole at the edge of the wood plank wall—a hole that had been clearly dug from the inside by someone trying to get out, not by an animal from the outside trying to get in.

The gap was fairly large, but not large enough for a person. Sonya hadn't succeeded.

Rafe bent over to inspect the bottom of the planks, some of them damaged. She bit her lip as she crouched next to him to see what he was looking at and spotted the dried blood. She could see in her mind Sonya trying to pull the boards loose until her fingertips bled. Isabelle's throat tightened.

"We'll find her." Rafe's voice sounded clipped as he straightened.

"Any idea where they've gone?" The sooner they started out, the better. No sense in wasting time here.

"Their tracks point south. We'll follow them." He was already heading for the door, which was stuck ajar, held in place by one of the crates he had moved there to let light in. He gave the crate a frustrated kick, sending it flying outside.

By pure chance she glanced up and saw something odd among the vines that grew on top of the hut and had sneaked inside, something that didn't belong there—a blue plastic-coated wire. Her brain moved faster than her eye. By the time she spotted the shapeless lump of plastic explosives she knew the hut had been booby-trapped.

"Bomb!" she yelled as she lurched forward.

Incomprehension flashed over Rafe's face even as he acted on reflex and grabbed for her, flung her from the hut in front of him, out toward safety. They didn't quite reach it. The next second the building blew, the force of the explosion lifting them both from the ground and sending them flying through the air.

Oh God, oh God, oh God. She flailed her arms as if that could slow her. Then she was smacking into the ground, hard. She couldn't breathe for a long moment. Everything hurt. Flaming boards rained from above. She covered her head, the most she could do. She didn't have it in her to try to crawl away.

After a few moments, once things quieted down, she looked up and spotted Rafe in the clearing smoke.

He wasn't moving.

"Rafe?" Odd, she could have sworn she spoke, but she could hear no sound coming out of her mouth. "Rafe?" she said louder, with the same result.

The explosion. Right. She was still deaf from it. She pulled herself up, did a routine check. What hurt? Everything. What broke? She tested her limbs. They all worked. Other than the scorch marks on her clothing and a few gaping tears here and there that revealed some serious abrasions, she seemed to be all right.

"Rafe?" She moved toward him, and over

the ringing in her ears she could finally hear something, a siren going off in the distance.

The explosion had been loud enough to be heard at the base. The Laderan military was about to come to investigate.

She hobbled toward Rafe, bent when she got there. "Get up." She grabbed his shoulder. "The soldiers are coming. We have to get out of here."

They didn't have time to deal with the army now. The questioning could last days. Two foreigners involved in a bombing incident next to a Laderan military base— they could be in jail for weeks before the U.S. consulate got them out. Sonya couldn't wait that long.

"Come on," she said, and felt panic rising from a deep, dark well inside when he didn't get up. How badly was he hurt?

He was lying on his back, moaning, or at least she thought he was. His lips were moving, his dark eyes rolled back in his head.

"Can you move?"

He blinked, focused on her, said something, repeated.

Am I dead? She read the words from his lips.

If he was joking, all was not yet lost. "Stop looking for the easy way out." She helped him sit, then slipped under his arm and pushed him up, carrying most of his weight.

When they were almost standing, he lurched forward, nearly sending both of them to the ground again. Maybe she couldn't do it. The panic was grabbing hold. What was she thinking? They both belonged on a stretcher.

Move. She struggled with the first step but managed without falling over. *Okay. One more.* Then another, then another. She dragged him like that to the edge of the woods. They'd rest later. Right now they had to find someplace to hide.

"Go," he said. "Leave me."

Now that his words vibrated inches from her ear, she could finally hear them.

He was in bad shape. It scared her breathless, but she couldn't show it. "Get moving, drama queen." She nudged him forward.

She didn't know what lay ahead, nor did she care, her only thought being to get as far away as possible from the army base and the soldiers who were coming after them.

"There." Rafe was pointing to an open

stretch of rocks to the left, the remnants of a landslide some time ago.

"No, not in the open." She ignored him and pulled him forward.

"Tracks," he said.

Where? She strained to see, then realized after a moment that he was talking about their tracks, the ones they were leaving behind. She glanced back. He was right; with both of them dragging their feet, they disturbed enough leaf mold that an idiot could follow them.

"Okay." She moved on toward the stony ground that wouldn't leave telltale signs of their passing.

They crossed that without trouble and made it into the woods again. Her legs wobbled. Rafe wasn't a small man. She couldn't support him like this for long.

He seemed to come to the same conclusion and pulled away from her. "Stop," he said and sank to the ground. "We'll rest a few minutes." The side of his face was covered with soot and blood. "How are you feeling?"

Her hearing was returning slowly. So far, so good. "Fine. You took the worst of the blast." At the last second he had positioned his body between hers and the hut. The thought brought an odd tightening sensation to her chest. She went down next to him and looked at a long cut on his neck that seemed the nastiest of his visible injuries. "Where else are you hurt? Is anything broken?"

"I don't think so. Just banged up pretty good." He drew a breath, let it out slowly. "I'm pretty sure this shoulder is dislocated." He nodded to the right.

She unbuttoned his ripped shirt and pulled it aside, stared at the bone that was clearly out of place.

No.

He couldn't be injured.

He was the only one between the two of them who knew what the hell they were doing out here. What did she know about the jungle? What did she know about Ladera? She needed him, needed his strength.

And he needed her.

"Okay. We'll fix it." She clenched her fists then unclenched them again, wiped her sweaty palms on her pants.

"Hold on to my hand," he said, sounding infinitely calmer than she felt.

She took his hand, squeezed it and felt a rush of doubt. "Maybe we could find a village doctor. You said there are some scattered villages on the hillside."

"Hold tight," he said and threw his body back.

The bone returned to its place with a crunching sound, ligaments snapping into place. His face went a sick ashen color for a moment.

Her stomach rolled over. Her muscles went weak. She took a deep breath then another as blood returned to her head.

"Thanks," he said, and tested the arm carefully before lifting her hand to his mouth and kissing it.

"Better?" She cleared her throat, ignoring the heat that skittered across her skin.

"Good as new." He smiled and seemed to regain color.

The relief that washed over her was short-lived. The sound of motors filtered through the woods.

"Four-wheelers," he said. "The soldiers use them to chase after drug traffickers. I bet the men who have Sonya got theirs from the base somehow."

It made sense. The vehicles fitted the terrain.

"We have to go." She stood and held out a hand to him.

"Thanks," he said, but stood without assistance. "I'm not that bad now. Just got my bones rattled around."

She glanced toward the base, the sound of motors growing louder. What now? The brief rest had helped, but still, neither of them were in the kind of shape it took to run. And even if they were, she doubted they could outrun the machines that were closing the distance behind them.

Chapter Three

His head was clearing finally, his body finding its way to working again. He still hurt all over, but at least he could walk on his own now, a step up from Isabelle having to help him.

Still, they were going too slow, and he couldn't pretend it wasn't him holding up the pace.

Rafe swallowed his frustration and pushed on.

They'd lucked out with the soldiers. The men had found the kidnappers' tracks and rushed off to follow those while he and Isabelle hid not three hundred feet from the hut.

"Let's stop to rest," she said, looking back at him, her concern for him easy to read in her eyes.

"No." He kept on going. "We'll stop at nightfall."

Darkness would be here soon enough, in an hour at the most.

They reached a small plateau covered by short trees and grasses. Above it on the other side where the land rose sharply, large trees reached for the sky, ninety or a hundred feet tall. The treetops were surrounded by mist, giving them an otherworldly appearance.

"How beautiful," she said with wonder in her voice when they reached the trees that towered to impossible heights above.

She stopped and was looking up at the trees with her head tilted, the muted light turning her strawberry-blond hair the color of antique gold. She looked like a wood sprite.

"Almost makes you believe in magic, doesn't it?" She looked at him and smiled that sweet, sexy smile of hers. "I swear I feel something. Like there's more here than just the trees."

He wouldn't have thought she, a foreigner, would pick up on that, and so fast. "The local tribes think so." He shrugged noncommittally and tried not to think of another time when he'd been alone in another cloud forest, doing something he shouldn't have been and had felt the anger of the woods.

Today the trees seemed welcoming in their majesty, Isabelle looking as if she'd always been here, as if she belonged. He watched the smile that played on her full lips and wanted her, in that moment, with unreasonable fierceness, to belong to him.

He caught himself stepping closer to her. Stopped.

This was nothing but an aftereffect of their close call with death. Something like that could make a person want to reach out and grab life with both hands. "We should go."

They crossed the woods, their trek feeling more like a dream than reality. He kept his GPS out and consulted it often now.

"Have you been here before?"

"Around," he said. "Not at this spot. My family is in Cedra, south of here."

"So what are we going to do now?" She voiced the question that had weighed heavily on his mind for the past couple of miles. "Should we see if we can pick up the kidnappers' trail?"

"The army would have ruined any usable tracks by now, looking for us." Their only lead had been obliterated.

"I'm not going back without Sonya."

In that, they agreed. Neither was he.

"The only two people we know for sure were involved with the kidnapping, Dr. Ramon and Fuentes, are both connected to Maggie. We need to talk to her."

"Ethan talked to her already. You saw the interview footage. She's locked up in a mental institute. I have a hard time seeing her orchestrating a complicated international kidnapping."

"But everything comes back to her."

"Not Juan's assassination attempt just a month ago. What if that and the kidnapping are connected?"

They kept coming back to the same argument over and over again. He kicked a fallen branch in frustration. There had to be something more, a clue they were missing.

Who had Sonya now?

"It comes down to your attitude about women, doesn't it?" she observed.

"I don't have an attitude about women. I like them."

"Exactly. You want to seduce them or protect them or both."

"What's wrong with that?" When it came to women, Ladera had very traditional family values.

"You don't want to persecute a woman. The thought of putting Maggie in jail makes you uncomfortable."

He hadn't really thought about it before, but she was right. The whole "pick on someone your own size" deal.

"This protection thing, it's not gentlemanly, you know."

"It isn't?" He was confused.

"It's an appendage of your chauvinistic predisposition."

"I'm not a chauvinist." He respected women, Isabelle being a prime example. She was as tough and as skilled as any man he'd ever known. He would have picked her to be on his team over anyone.

"So you want to protect women because they are the *stronger* sex?" She drew up an eyebrow.

He didn't have a ready response for that.

She didn't seem to mind the wait.

"It's just… I mean, if anyone needs help and I'm in a position to give help, I should give it."

"Do you trust me?"

The question surprised him. "Of course. But if you think I'm going to let you step in front of a bullet and do nothing about it, you have another thing coming."

"But you don't trust my instincts?"

Not about Maggie. Not when they went against his own. That would have been blind trust, and blind trust required taking someone's word and following it, jumping without looking. He had learned early on that kind of trust could get a man killed faster than most anything.

And yet, if he were to trust someone completely, blindly, it would have been Isabelle. She was as sharp and as competent as they came. There was something in her, a tenacious quest for truth and justice that he recognized as part of what made him tick as well, that was the cornerstone of his newly built life. It put them on the same wavelength.

If she was certain, if she was absolutely sure

about Maggie, he owed it to her to give it some more thought.

"Okay," he said.

"Okay, what?" She turned to look at him.

"While Rachel is searching for more information on Dr. Ramon and Maggie's cousin, we'll stop by and check out the ex-Mrs. DeLeon."

She flashed him a brilliant smile. "Thanks."

He nodded.

They walked on, each step requiring effort as the elevation rose. Hour after hour passed. They didn't talk much, conserving energy. Dusk was settling on the forest by the time they came to a break in the woods. The mountainside in front of them was green with moss, but, higher above, snow capped the peaks. At least that wasn't something they had to worry about. They would be going around the base of the mountain.

"Look." She stopped and pointed.

He moved his hand closer to his gun as he stepped in front of her and watched the dark spots in the green. They didn't seem to be moving. He looked harder and realized they were larger than man-size, much larger.

"Rocks." He relaxed.

"I think they're caves," she said.

Hard to tell in the twilight, but maybe she was right. He stared at the largest one, tried to detect the way the shadows fell. "Let's check them out." A warm shelter would be a great find for the upcoming night.

They were only halfway up the hill when darkness fell, making the rest of the way a slower journey. They both had flashlights, but neither reached for them, making do with whatever light the moon provided. If anyone was out there in the surrounding woods, Isabelle and he would make an easy mark on the open hillside.

Few trees grew here and those that did were much shorter than the giants of the cloud forest. What shrubs they came across they went around—faster that way than trying to clear a path with the machete.

He looked up, checking the distance to the cave, and slipped back a foot or so when small stones shifted under his boots. "Watch out." He looked back to make sure she saw where the bad patch was and avoided it.

They were coming to a section of gravel,

covered with moss here and there, much larger stones interspersed with the small.

"It's almost like steps," Isabelle said and stopped to look closer.

Twisting his body to shield the light, he turned on his flashlight and pointed the beam in front of their feet. "We might have come across some ancient ruins."

He clicked off the light and continued upward, following the steps that in places were completely covered with vegetation, in other spots had large chunks missing. They followed them and reached the first opening in the hillside. Instead of the cave they had expected, it turned out to be a stone doorway carved in breathtaking detail, the images soft-edged, worn down by the weather, looking like a low-resolution art photograph.

"Wow. Did we discover something?" She was staring at the carvings, running her finger down the likeness of a man in a feather hat.

"I don't think so. The Inca ruins in Ladera are fairly well cataloged. They're all over the mountain."

"Why aren't there tourists here? It's beautiful."

"It's probably not one of the larger or more preserved sites. And it's out in the middle of nowhere. Shall we go in?" He flicked on his flashlight. As long as they pointed the beam forward and blocked the back with their bodies, they should be okay, and after they progressed a few yards, they'd be in far enough not to be seen.

She switched on her own light and scanned the walls, decorated by more carvings, perfectly preserved in some spots, nearly obliterated by weather and wild animals in other places. The corridor was about four feet wide and eight feet high, splitting into three branches after a short while. Two of the hallways were collapsed. They followed the third and disturbed a couple of bats, who flew overhead and out into the night.

A room opened to the left, about ten by ten, rounded. The floor was littered with old bones of every shape and size.

Isabelle stepped closer to him. "What is it?" she asked, her voice thinner than usual.

"A jaguar's den," he said, and bent down to look at a small skull.

She was so close now she was touching him. "Maybe we shouldn't be here."

He felt a moment of temptation to play up the danger and keep her glued to him all night, but he straightened. "What do you smell?"

She sniffed. "Dust and stale air."

"If a big cat still lived here, you'd be able to smell it all the way from the entrance. Remember what it's like in the zoo next to the lions' cages?"

She nodded, her shoulders relaxing.

"They're nearly extinct. Running into one is the least of our worries." He scanned the room.

"So what is this place? Other than an abandoned jaguar den."

"No idea. It is a religious site, though, and not just some palace."

"How do you know?"

"The round walls. The Incas only used them in their temples."

They moved on, finding more forking hallways, rooms large and small, more curves.

"Better start backing out before we get lost," he said after a while. They'd seen enough rooms to ensure that no drug runners were holed up in there for the night. "We'll sleep closer to the entrance."

"In here we could start a fire. Nobody would see," she said.

The idea was tempting, the chill of night already in the air, but they had other things to consider.

"We could get trapped too easily. I want a spot from where I can see the hillside."

When they reached the opening, she laid out their sleeping bags. He unpacked the food.

"I suppose even a small fire would be too risky," she said when they were done. "You think the army will find us?"

"Not tonight. But the army is not our only worry. Other people walk in these woods. The kind of men we wouldn't want to meet."

"People who traffic drugs?"

"That." He fell silent for a moment. "And poachers," he added. "There are also a couple of outfits that are involved in illegal logging. Any of these would think we might be here spying on them. They don't like to leave witnesses."

They ate their cold rations in silence.

When he looked up between two bites, he

caught her shivering. The temperature had to be in the low forties, but seemed even colder because of the wind. They really did need something warm. He took his chunk of aged cheese with him and stepped outside, gathered an armful of wood.

"Watch the hillside," he said, then grabbed his backpack and went into the temple.

"WHAT'S THAT?" Isabelle asked when he came out about twenty minutes later with their traveling cups in his hands.

He was tall and wide-shouldered and handsome, all rumpled from the danger they'd just been through, standing in the hall of a breathtaking ancient ruin, looking very Indiana Jones-ish.

Her heart rate picked up when he held out one of the cups to her with a smile.

"Yerba maté. A kind of tea the natives drink. I got it at that market we stopped by. Try it."

She did, warmth spreading to her hands from the cup, then through her body as she swallowed. She must have made a face at the taste because his smile turned into a teasing grin.

"That bad, huh? I should have warned you. It's herbal tea."

"That explains the taste," she said, but took another mouthful and another, enjoying the warmth the tea brought to her body. "Does it do anything?"

"Supposedly everything," he said with a measure of skepticism. "If you ask the old folks they tell you it's good for health, vigor and endurance among a host of other things. Drinking the maté is a kind of institution in Ladera." He sipped his own cup. "I missed it."

"What else did you miss?"

"If you go in there, the fire is still going. You can get warmed up," he said as he sat down. "I'll keep watch."

And because she did need the heat, she didn't ask her question again or wonder too much about why he hadn't answered.

She found the fire in the jaguar's den and sat next to it, grateful that Rafe had pushed all the bones in a pile by the wall. The small room was decorated with carvings from the floor to the ceiling, as far up as the fire illuminated the walls—abstract shapes, geometric forms, highly stylized animal figures.

She drank her tea and relaxed in the warmth of the fire, let her eyes drift closed after a while. It had been a difficult day. She thought of the explosion, of the earthquake. What if— The thought pushed her to her feet and sent her scrambling to the entrance, to Rafe.

"What if there's another quake? Should we be in here?"

"It's probably the safest place." He pointed to the large boulder of the doorway above his head. "Inca builders had centuries worth of experience with earthquakes. They built for it."

He was probably right. She sank to her sleeping bag next to him, some of the tension seeping out of her body. "I'll watch next. You go warm up."

"I'm okay," he said. "You can go back if you'd like."

But she stayed where she was, comforted by his company and lost in the incredible beauty that stretched before them in the moonlight—the ruins, the trees, the sky dotted with a million stars that seemed within arm's reach.

She looked down the narrow steps that had brought them here. "Had to be hard for the

Incas to cart everything they needed up here for the temple."

"They didn't cart. They carried. Well, they and their llamas and alpacas. They never invented the wheel."

"You're kidding." She looked around with new appreciation. The sheer effort it must have taken to maintain the temple, not to mention large Inca cities, without something as basic as the wheel boggled the mind.

"The archeologists say the Inca never had a written language, either. At least, not one that's been discovered so far."

"Hard to picture them running an empire without record keeping."

He nodded.

"How do you know so much about them, anyhow?"

"When I was a kid, I worked for a team of Mexican archeologists one summer. I crawled into places no one could fit, that kind of work."

That had to be awesome, being let loose in the woods, being part of an archeological excavation. The most excitement she'd had as a kid was going to Grandma's house. Her brothers were the ones getting caught up in all the wild stuff and getting into trouble. "You must have had so much fun."

He shrugged. "If you don't mind snakes, scorpions and poisonous spiders."

She glanced at the floor and pulled closer to him. She really hated bugs, would have taken on armed conflict instead of having to deal with a centipede any day.

"Scared?" he baited her.

She wasn't exactly scared, just very, very uncomfortable at the thought of anything crawling on her. Growing up with four brothers had toughened her up in most regards, but in this one she managed to preserve her girlishness in full. "No."

"So, if you have to go to the bathroom in the middle of the night, you're going without me?" He raised a dark eyebrow.

"Absolutely not," she said and tried to put a spin on it. "I wouldn't leave you alone here, unprotected. We're a team. We should stick together."

A smile hovered over his lips. "You need me. Admit it."

She did need him, no doubt about that. She remembered the panic she'd felt in that split second after the explosion when she'd thought he might have been dead. They brought different skills to the mission. She needed his knowledge of the woods, the country. And beyond that, she needed his company.

"I do need you," she said. She was mature enough to admit it.

Heat flared in his eyes.

"I meant it in a professional sense," she added, feeling warm all of a sudden.

Their closeness in the past couple of days was getting to her. They were forever touching, pulling each other across ditches, over fallen trees. They'd slept side by side. The effect his body was having on hers seemed harder and harder to ignore.

Her problem, she thought. She was not going to make a fool out of herself by throwing herself at him like half the women in Miami.

"Mmm." He drew lines in the dust at his feet but didn't take his gaze off her. "I need you, too. Thanks for helping me after the explosion."

"That's why I'm here," she said nonchalantly, but the warmth inside her spread. She sipped her tea, staying quiet. They sat face-to-face, barely separated by a few inches.

The adrenalin rush of the day still hummed in her blood.

She dropped her gaze from his. It settled on the dry blood on his neck.

"Let me take a look at your injuries," she said a moment before it registered that touching him was the last thing she should be doing if she hoped to regain some peace of mind.

She pulled her last clean T-shirt from her bag and wet it from her aluminum flask she'd refilled from a stream they'd passed along the way. She started with his forehead. Safe enough as long as she didn't look into those swirling chocolate eyes that watched her.

She cleared her throat. "Turn your head this way."

She dabbed at the dry blood on his neck gently, not wanting the wound to start bleeding again. "This should have stitches." But there was nothing to be done for it here. He was going to have a hell of a scar.

"Damn, I'm getting old," he said when she was done, and rolled his neck with a sour smile. "I used to take beatings better."

She watched him in the moonlight. He didn't look old, despite the few strands of gray that were coming out at his temple. He looked very masculine in a distinguished kind of way, and extremely sexy.

"You know, when you said *bomb*, I thought…we might…" He shook his head and reached out to touch the side of her face where she'd bruised the skin. And before she could react, he was already leaning over, his lips hovering over the bruise, then brushing it slowly, gently.

The flood tide of sensations caught her off guard.

Instinct warred with instinct inside her— one to turn her head and match her lips to his to drown in him, the other to pull back and save herself.

He couldn't have meant it as anything more than a friendly gesture. He'd pull away in a second.

But he didn't. God help her, he lingered.

And then he shifted to her mouth, while she sat there unable to move.

Rafe Montoya was kissing her.

Her brain was flashing the thought in neon lights while it shut down all other cerebral activity.

His lips were warm and supple and gentle, and they felt better than any fantasy she'd ever entertained about the man.

She moaned—might have been a whimper for mercy—and he took advantage of it to taste her fully. Man, oh man, he could kiss. He was tender but thorough, each second taking her closer and closer to the melting point.

By the time he pulled away, she was a puddle at his feet.

Somewhere in the back of her mind it registered that he was breathing just as hard as she was, looked just as dazed as she felt.

"You have no idea how long I've wanted to do that," he said. "You're not going to shoot me tomorrow on the trail for this, are you?" He tried to go for the light teasing tone but didn't quite pull it off.

She didn't trust herself to speak, so she nodded. Damn right she was going to have something to say about this. They were colleagues. What had he been thinking?

"I thought so. Better make it worthwhile then," he said with a devastating smile and pulled her into his arms.

She lifted her head so their lips would meet sooner.

"Why haven't we done this before?" he asked the next time they came up for air.

"We work together?" she said weakly.

"I don't think Rachel would fire us for being happy."

He had a point there. Of course there had to be a hundred other reasons why this was not a good idea. She could remember having a whole list of them at one point; right now, however, she couldn't recall any. "Maybe one more kiss," she said. "In the interest of keeping each other warm."

He grinned. "Exactly what I've been thinking."

And of course he'd lied, because from the way he kissed her it was as obvious as the moon in the sky that he'd been thinking about a lot more than just a kiss.

His hands ran down her arms and up her waist, his long fingers stroking her until, frustrated, she pulled her shirt out of her waistband to let him in.

She wanted his hands on her, she had wanted this forever. So why not have it, for a moment or two? It wasn't as if anything else could happen between them here on the hillside tonight. It seemed safe to play just a little. After the day they'd had, they both deserved a little tenderness and some release of tension.

The warmth of his palm on her naked skin brought a breathtaking jolt of pleasure. Then he moved up, until the tip of his fingers grazed the underside of her breasts. He held still, driving her crazy with anticipation. She waited for an eternity; her breath caught in her throat. And then he cupped her.

She could feel her nipples strain against him and the friction drove her crazy. *More, more, more.* She'd been dreaming about this for too long, denied it too long to stop it now, even if he was all wrong for her. For the first time in her well-ordered, rational life, she didn't care.

Sometimes a woman just had to say to hell with the consequences.

His hands on her, his lips, unleashed something primal, a need that went so deep it scared her.

He helped her out of her sweater and shirt,

tugged aside her bra and took a hardened nipple into his mouth—progressing with breathtaking speed. The contrast between the heat of his tongue and the cool air on her skin was exquisitely erotic. The geometric images carved into the doorway seemed to swirl above them.

She wanted more and wanted it now. She tugged off his sweater, and he shrugged off his shirt, impatient. His bruises looked darker in the moonlight. And she remembered how in that last second before the bomb blew, instead of jumping clear, he had reached back for her to pull her from the hut where she would have been blown to pieces.

"Wait. Wait." She gasped for air and sanity. "We can't. You're hurt."

"So are you," he said, his head about level with her navel. He was looking at her abrasions.

"It's fine," she said, but he was already going for the water to wash them, then smoothed some of his miracle ointment into her roughed-up skin so gently that she barely felt it.

"Better?" he asked.

She nodded, the breath catching in her

throat as his fingers moved on to knead the healthy parts in a sensuous massage. Still sitting, he pulled her into his lap, straddling him, and buried his face between her aching breasts. Heat spread up and through her from his hardness, which strained between her legs.

This would be a good point to stop, she thought hazily, but couldn't bring herself to interrupt him just yet. The lack of protection would stop them soon, anyway. There was only so far they could go. Rather than frustrating, the idea comforted her like a safety net. Things couldn't get out of hand. They were both adults and responsible enough.

Her hands skimmed over his shoulders, and he lifted her in order to reach more of her with his mouth.

"Regaining strength, are you?" she teased, breathless.

"I had plenty of yerba maté." He brushed her fevered skin with his lips. "Didn't I tell you it works wonders?"

Need throbbed between her legs.

She pushed him onto his back, onto one of the sleeping bags, kissed the base of his throat and moved lower, covering his warm skin with her lips, moving inch by inch until she found his pebbled nipple among a smattering of silky hair.

"I should have got blown up sooner," he said, sounding gratifyingly weak.

She looked up. "Don't think I'm going to do this every time you get friendly with a bomb." He had to be discouraged from reckless action.

He flashed a smile and pulled her up until their lips met, flipped her under him and kissed her with so much heated passion it shook loose something deep inside her. Desire curled with sharp heat at the V of her thighs, and he was doing his best to get to it, working on her pants. She shifted to make his job easier.

He stripped them off then pulled up her knees and spread them, ran his fingers lightly over her skin from her ankle to the top. He caressed one inner thigh while kissing the other, then switched, tasting, nibbling, driving her crazy.

He was maddeningly slow and careful and thorough. How could he not feel the urgency that gripped her, that pulled her forward faster and faster?

She hadn't planned to come this far. She'd planned on stopping right after some kissing, right after she'd finally run her fingers over his well-toned body, right after she had a long-lusted-after taste of his skin.

But now she wanted it all, wanted it with a desperation—full release.

He reached for her underwear and it sobered her a little.

She put a hand over his to stop him even as her body howled in disbelief and disappointment. "We should—"

"Right." He seemed to pull back with an effort. "I was going to." He reached over her, back toward his pack and after a moment came up with a small foil package.

"You planned this?" she asked, stunned, her mind reeling while her body screamed, *yes! yes! yes!*

"Not exactly." He had an endearingly embarrassed expression on his face. "But I did give some thought to going on a trip with the sexiest woman I know, a woman I happen to have had the hots for these past three tantalizing years." He took a slow breath. "I told myself I wasn't going to touch you if you fell on top of me naked. It wouldn't be right. Then I dropped the box in. There was no plan. I swear," he said, and looked sincerely frustrated as he dragged his fingers through his hair. "See? This is what I mean when I say you drive me crazy."

And she did see, right on the edge of insanity as his hardness touched against her belly while he waited for her response.

"I want you," he said, looking her straight in the eye. "I've wanted you for a long time. But this only works if you feel the same."

Her body hummed with arousal and need, her nipples hard spikes, her underwear damp. He only had to look at her to know how much she wanted him. It felt useless and stupid to lie.

"Yes," she said.

The next second his lips were over hers and he was kissing her with an intensity that erased any further thought from her mind.

He was drawing some tantalizing pattern on her skin around her underwear, tugging at the small triangle of cloth an inch, going back to play, tugging another inch. She reached for his pants and underwear and pushed them down in one smooth move.

"In a hurry?" he asked against her lips.

"Yes." She kissed him as she ran her hands over his firm buttocks, smiled when she heard the breath catch in his throat.

"What happened to savoring the—" he said a moment later but fell suddenly silent as she lifted her hips.

"Sorry. We're going to savor next time." He lifted his gaze to hers and made quick work of protection. "Mission's engaged. I'm going in," he said a moment later, just before he claimed her lips.

She arched her back as his swollen tip rubbed against her entrance. Control over the situation, over her body was slipping away fast, but she felt content to let it go.

When he pushed inside her, the explosion of pleasure that shook her took her breath away.

He gave a soft laugh as she looked at him, stunned.

"Again," he said, and pulled out slowly then pushed back in.

It was too much, too fast. Her body had to come down from the first high. She was still contracting around him for heaven's sake. She couldn't again. Not yet.

But the pressure turned up and kept building anew, and he proved to her that she could.

"Satisfied?" he asked a while later when he lay lazily next to her, watching her face, running his fingers down her cheek to brush her hair back.

"Wrung out, used up, an empty shell," she said, her bones feeling liquefied.

"Me, too," he said and pulled her into his arms as he lay back.

Her head rested on his hard-muscled chest, the scent of his warm skin enveloping her in a haze of contentment.

"You sleep, I'll keep watch," he said.

"Mmm. Wake me for my turn." She stretched against him like a cat.

"Keep that up," he warned, "and neither of us will get any sleep."

The prospect seemed thrilling. But in the interest of their mission, she put herself on her best behavior.

Chapter Four

He'd had three life-defining moments in his forty years, and he could recall all three with clarity. The first was when he'd been recruited by one of the drug bosses for trafficking at the age of ten and was able to save his family from starvation. The second came at twenty-five when a rival, Ricky Mentina, decided to take him out at his niece's christening. God in his mercy saw to it that none of his family had got hurt. The incident sobered him out enough to realize he had to leave that life before his dealings hurt someone he loved—a decision that eventually led to his job with Miami Confidential as an undercover agent. The third defining moment had been making love to Isabelle on the hillside.

He was pretty sure this one was going to change his life just as drastically as the first two.

Because now that they'd crossed the line, there was no way in hell they could go back to being just co-workers again. No way he could ever look at her and not see her with her face flushed as she threw back her head and moaned with pleasure beneath him.

She slowed and he caught up with her, catching that light orange scent that clung to her skin and drew him. He shook his head lightly. He'd been done in by citrus.

They were just a few miles outside of Capunata, a midsized miner town on the plateau where he planned to buy or rent a car that would take them south to Maggie DeLeon.

"At one point, before we go back, we should…" She avoided looking at him. "We should discuss what happened."

Frustration nipped at him. He waited a beat as they walked. "By discussing, I assume you mean come to a mutual agreement that it had been a mistake and assure each other that it will never happen again." His blood stirred.

"It's not that—"

"Isabelle." He stopped her and turned her

gently to face him. "You are an intelligent woman. You had to know that I've wanted you for a very long time."

Her face turned a shade pinker as she twisted from him and walked on, picking up pace, her stride full of strength yet graceful—the two best adjectives to describe her as a whole. "This is not helping," she said.

"Because you're approaching it like a woman."

Her eyes flashed as she turned back. "And how is that?"

Okay. He was going to treat this lightly for now, give her time to get used to the idea. "In situations like this, women want to discuss things. Men just want to do it again, as soon as possible. You know, men are very simple creatures really. I mean, we were good together, phenomenal. We are two consenting adults. What is there to discuss?"

"I'm not the kind of woman who indiscriminately flitters from one affair to the next." Her voice was thick with reproach.

No, she wasn't that kind of a woman. Which was why he had told himself to keep his hands off her in the past. She deserved better than what he could give. Except now—

He had gone and done it, got involved with her. There would be no good way, no easy way out this time—not with a woman like Isabelle Rush. And, to his surprise, he found that he wasn't actually looking for a way out just yet. He was still looking for a way further in.

He wanted to get to know her better. Beyond the job.

The thought stopped him. They had worked together for years. He knew her a hell of a lot better than any woman he had ever dated.

He caught up with her easily. "I'm not a womanizer," he said, and when she made some small sound, he added, "I'm not a monk, either."

"I've noticed," she said drily. "We've all noticed."

The way she said those words stung a little. He'd thought he had kept his private life private. He hadn't paraded his dates at Weddings Your Way. Then again, neither had he kept it a secret when he went out. He had a lot of casual acquaintances in the Laderan community in Miami and somebody was always putting something on, inviting him. He enjoyed the familiar food, the familiar music, the understanding that came from being among people who came from similar beginnings as he had, speaking the language he'd grown up with.

He usually had a date, not that he went out of his way to get one. He knew a lot of beautiful Laderan-American women and a lot of times it made sense to go with someone rather than alone. They might have danced and flirted, kissed, touched. But more often than not, the night had ended at the lady's doorstep; rarely did he go beyond. He didn't live a celibate life, but neither had he ever lived up to his reputation.

"You should understand. We travel, we target the bad guys and we're the target for them. We lie about who we are, what we do." How on earth was he supposed to bring somebody permanently into that? "I like good food, good wine, good company. Nothing wrong with that. I never promised anything to anyone. I was looking for entertainment. The people I spent time with were looking for the same," he said to reassure himself, then grinned at her. "Of course, things get exaggerated with the guys at the office. You shouldn't take that seriously."

"Whatever you say. It's all right. It doesn't really matter."

What didn't matter? His past or what had happened between them at the temple? He was pretty sure she was talking about the latter.

"The hell it doesn't. It matters to me."

And just how much it mattered was somewhat alarming. What the hell was wrong with him?

"So you picture this, how?" Her eyes glinted hard. "At work we pretend nothing happened and every couple of days we get together for an hour or so in the evening at your bachelor pad?"

Normally, that would have worked just beautifully for him. With Isabelle, a relationship of that kind seemed neither possible nor satisfactory. He tried to picture it, had no trouble with the lovemaking part, but the rest wouldn't gel. He wanted more.

He wanted to take her out on the bay on the boat he'd recently bought and had told no one about. Why? He had specifically bought the boat as a haven, a place where nobody could just drop in on him.

But all of a sudden solitude on the water didn't seem half as appealing as time with Isabelle.

"I think…" He took a deep breath. "I want a relationship." The words that had come out of his mouth left him bewildered.

They seemed to have the same effect on Isabelle.

She stopped and was staring at him. Some emotion flashed across her face but was gone before he could identify it.

"How hard did you hit your head in that explosion?"

"Come on, Isabelle," he said, but couldn't entirely blame her for not taking him seriously. He himself had trouble believing what was happening to him.

"It's the whole midlife crisis thing, isn't it?" she asked.

Was it? Her words had a considerable cooling effect.

He'd turned forty a few months before. He was in Ladera where you weren't a man until you had a wife and a houseful of children. And he was back here with a beautiful woman he'd been lusting after for years. Maybe his subconscious mind was putting two and two together.

Rafe relaxed. Maybe that was it. Maybe it would go away. If not sooner, then when he returned to Miami, to his normal surroundings.

"There's a path up ahead," Isabelle said, and moved ahead, effectively ending the conversation.

Just as well. He needed time to think. "Let's follow it. It'll come out somewhere above town. They're going to see us anyway. We'll walk out of the woods like a pair of hikers."

Following the well-used path was a blessing. He could tuck away the machete and the GPS at last. They walked in silence. By midmorning, they could see the end of the trees; then they were out in the open, on the outskirts of Capunata.

Small wood homes edged the town, leaning against taller and better kept neighbors. They could look down the main street from where they were, at the line of stores and two churches—both of them Catholic.

Other than the few beat-up cars and pickups parked on the streets, the place reminded him of the Old West.

Close to a hundred people were gathered to their right at the edge of town, going about with carts, women with baskets on their heads.

"Market day." He looked over the stalls and their colorful array of wares. Perfect. That much easier to blend in to the crowd, replenish their supplies and find transportation that would take them south.

He headed toward one of the *parrillas,* a shack that sold grilled food. They were both ready to have a warm meal. Saliva gathered in his mouth at the smell of spicy *carne asada.* But before they got anywhere near nourishment, a police officer stepped out of the crowd in front of them.

"Buenos días Señor y Señorita. Documentos, por favor," the man said in a friendly tone. He looked very much like one of the locals, his position indicated only by the badge on his hat and the gun belt around his waist.

Checking people's IDs at random wasn't something Laderan police did routinely. Why had they been singled out? Rafe looked around, uneasy, but didn't see another officer.

Isabelle was already handing over her passport with a smile. He did the same, hoping to get away from the man quickly.

The man flipped through the pages. "Americans. Welcome to Capunata. There was some trouble up the mountain. We must check everyone who comes in from that direction," he said in heavily accented English. "Would you come with me?"

"We are just tourists. We haven't seen anything suspicious up there," Rafe responded. "Is anything out of order with our papers?"

"No, nothing, *señor.* Just a formality. The captain wants to personally look at everyone who is from out of the country."

He glanced around again, judged their chances of dodging the man and making it into the woods. They could do it. Probably. The policeman would shoot, of course. He watched the children who played catch, dashing in and out of the crowd, then looked at the man again, who already had their passports tucked away in his breast pocket.

If they ran, they had to do it now. Of

course, within minutes both the army and the police would be in pursuit. Having to hide from them, having to trek back maybe to lose them, lying low for days perhaps... No, they couldn't afford to waste that much time. Better to chance the captain.

Nothing could tie them to the explosion at the army base. Their papers were in perfect order. In all probability the interview would be over in minutes and end in apologies for causing them delay.

Rafe set aside his misgivings and nodded to Isabelle, and when the man started forward they followed him.

The police station was only a couple hundred yards away, a one-story building with peeling masonry and a steel-reinforced door that led straight to the booking area. Two other officers lounged in the room, viewing Rafe and Isabelle with interest. The man who'd brought them in walked behind the counter.

"I'll need your backpacks. Please empty your pockets."

"Are we being arrested?" Isabelle asked. "For what? You said we would just have to speak to the captain."

"No arrest. You go into holding until the captain can talk to you. It's our procedure."

Like hell they would. Rafe stepped forward. Isabelle must have seen the fight in his eyes because she put a hand on his arm before he could open his mouth.

"Okay. That's fine," she said to the officer.

She was right. They couldn't get into a scuffle with the police. Better to play by their rules if that got them out faster. But letting someone lock him up went against every instinct he had.

IT WASN'T JUST THE AIR that stunk—the floor, the walls, the bench she refused to sit on, they all reeked, the mixture of vomit, sweat and urine thick in the air. Isabelle cupped her nose and closed her eyes, careful not to sway against the wall.

At least she wasn't bored. She took turns despairing over the fact that they were in jail, their mission having come to a grinding halt, and obsessing over what had happened between Rafe and her on the hillside and their talk on the way down.

He wanted a *relationship*.

She was pretty sure the only reason he used the word was because he didn't know what it meant.

Footsteps scuffed the chipped tile floor, the sound nearing. She opened her eyes.

"Las manos, por favor."

A second passed before she figured out what the guard wanted. She stuck her hands through the bars, and he slapped the cuffs on then opened the door and let her out.

He took her past two empty cells before turning down a narrow hallway. She glanced at the beat-up phone screwed to the wall, but before she could ask to make a call the man stopped and rapped on the second door on the right. It opened immediately.

She stepped in after him and looked around the small office as the door closed behind her. Another uniformed guard stood by the wall inside. A middle-aged, scrawny-looking man sat behind a metal desk, blending into the dirty gray paint that covered the walls. His small brown eyes brimmed with mistrust as they darted over her.

"Buenos días, señorita."

"Buenos días, señor." She kept her voice respectful.

Everything she'd ever heard about South American prisons crowded into her mind now. There were three guards, at least two armed—she couldn't see if the man behind the desk had a gun but probably so. She glanced around for anything she could use as a weapon if things went bad and she had to defend herself, cuffed as she was.

The few file folders on the desk didn't look promising. She glanced at the dusty aluminum fan in the window. Rafe would have been so much better at this. Before coming to Miami Confidential, she was a criminologist, for heaven's sake, an academic for all intents and purposes.

"I'm Julio Hernandez, the police captain, Señorita Rush. Please take a seat," the captain said in pretty good English, and one of his men immediately pulled out a cane chair for her.

So far so good. She sat, still tense, but cautiously hopeful.

"Thank you." She smiled at the captain. "I was hoping we would be able to talk. It seems there is a misunderstanding—"

He held up a hand, cutting her off. "What are you doing in Ladera?"

She didn't like the way he looked her over, but she kept her face and voice polite. "I am the spokesperson for Weddings Your Way, the company that is organizing Señor Juan DeLeon's wedding."

"And Señor DeLeon plans his honeymoon in Capunata?"

His voice mocked her, but she didn't care. As long as they were just talking, she was prepared to put up with any insult he threw her way. She kept the smile plastered on her face. "As you probably saw in the papers, Señor DeLeon's fiancée has been kidnapped in the United States."

The man nodded.

"I came with a colleague to visit Señor DeLeon's family and also to give a press conference since the planned wedding was receiving so much attention in the media."

"I understand Mr. Montoya works security. You did not feel safe coming alone?"

If he knew that, it meant Rafe had already been interrogated. She focused on the story they had agreed on ahead of time, made sure there wouldn't be any discrepancies.

"He is working closely with the Miami police. He came to answer any questions the family might have about the status of the investigation."

The man waited a few beats.

"And you were in the mountains, why exactly?"

"Mr. Montoya was born in Ladera," she said. The captain would know as much from Rafe's passport already. "He promised to show me some of the country while we were here." It certainly sounded logical and reasonable. She couldn't see how the man could find fault with that. Thousands of tourists poured into Ladera each year to hike in the Andes.

"Army bases?" He drew up a bushy eyebrow.

"We went to see the cloud forest."

"Did you see or hear anything suspicious?" He was watching her closely, his small eyes narrowed. "Did you meet with anyone else while you were up there?"

"No one. We went on a short hike, that's all. It's a beautiful place. I've never seen anything like it. I'm glad I got the chance."

"You were both armed." His voice was cold. His face said he wasn't buying any of her innocent enthusiasm.

"We had some concerns about running into smugglers. The papers are full of stories."

He stared at her for a few seconds then looked down, shuffled some papers and took off his flat-top hat, smoothed his comb-over into place with his fingers.

"Are you aware that there was an explosion near where you hiked?"

"An explosion?" She did her best to look confused. "Loggers? We saw some cleared areas as we walked."

"You seem to have some bruises. Señor Montoya has injuries as well."

Oh, God, she hadn't thought of that. Did he ask Rafe the same thing? What had Rafe said? "Hiking," she smiled. "We both slipped a few times. And that earthquake caught us in the wrong spot—too many falling trees and branches."

He watched her in silence.

"We do have a tight schedule, *señor*," she said after a while. "Would you be able to—"

"There's nothing I can do. A military

officer is coming down from the base to interrogate everyone who was detained on suspicion. He is stopping in each town on the way. He might be here tomorrow or the day after."

Too long. They didn't have that much time. She sweetened her smile. "I'm sure you have the authority to eliminate suspects like us who so obviously have nothing to do with the incident."

He didn't seem impressed. "The order is to hold all detainees until further notice."

Great. "How many detainees do you have?" she asked out of curiosity.

"Just the two of you so far." He seemed disappointed as he said that.

"There have been many arrests in the surrounding towns?" She was hoping to figure out how many interviews that military officer would have to conduct before he got to them.

"Dozens." He put his hat back on. "Thank you for your cooperation, Señorita Rush." He nodded toward the door and one of his men opened it while the other grabbed her elbow and escorted her forward.

"I'm happy to help any way I can," she called back before the door closed behind her.

She looked at the phone on the wall within hands reach. *"Por favor, señor?"*

"¿Querría usted utilizar el teléfono?"

"Sí, señor. Muchas gracias."

He didn't let her go even as she reached for the receiver. Fine. She dialed Rachel's cell as fast as she could, in case the captain came out and decided that allowing her use of the phone wasn't such a great idea. Rafe, when he got the chance to call, would try for the American embassy. That way, they'd have their bases covered. Those were about all the plans they'd been able to make before they'd been separated.

"Weddings Your Way, Rachel…" The familiar voice with its slight Colorado flavor brought a pang of comfort.

"It's Isabelle, listen—"

"Where have you two been? We've been trying to reach you. Why aren't your phones turned on?"

"We are in jail." She cut to the chase, unsure how much time the guard would allow her.

There was a moment of silence on the other end of the line.

"How bad? Did Rafe kill anyone?"

"No." Not yet, although during the arrest when their backpacks had been taken away, she'd at one point thought he would go for the arresting officer who'd shoved her. "There was an explosion in the mountains. We were at the wrong place at the wrong time." She didn't dare say more. Although none of the guards had spoken English to her so far, she couldn't be sure they didn't understand it.

"Are you okay?"

"We're both fine. We are in some local jail in Capunata."

"I'll have our lawyer start working on it immediately."

"Thanks."

The guard was nudging her.

"I better go."

"We're going to get you out. Take care of yourself, okay? Stay safe."

"Thanks Rachel."

"*¿Quiere usar el baño?*" the man asked as he walked her back.

"*No necesito, gracias.*" They'd let her go to

the bathroom before they'd locked her up, although *bathroom* wasn't the right word for the pit of despair, stinky and dirty, the lidless bowls chipped and stained. She wasn't desperate enough yet for another trip.

She walked back to her cell, held her hands out for the man to take the cuffs off, went straight to the spot where she could feel a little movement of air from a window that was open somewhere down the hall.

Lying down for a while would have been nice. She looked at the bench and considered it for a second but ended up squatting instead, her arms folded over her knees. She wished they hadn't separated her from Rafe. His presence would have helped pass the time.

He couldn't be far. As far as she could tell, the jail consisted of one long hallway with cells of various sizes opening off of it. Had he had a chance to call the embassy? He was probably plotting escape by now. She smiled at the thought, then grew serious again when it occurred to her that he might have received a different treatment than the one she'd been given. Would they be rougher on him because he was a man?

He was still not one hundred percent, due to the explosion, although he was quickly recovering. She hoped he had cooperated and gave no reason to anyone to use unnecessary roughness.

About an hour passed. She stood to stretch her legs. Another hour went by, and despite the stench all around her, she felt the first pangs of hunger. What time was it? She figured late afternoon but couldn't be sure. They'd taken her watch.

The footsteps came again. Food. It had to be food. Or if not that, at least water. She hadn't had a drop since that morning and was prepared to drink whatever they brought her, risking diarrhea and parasites.

Her shoulders slumped when the guard who walked into view came empty-handed.

"*Venga esta saliendo,*" he said. *You're leaving.*

Leaving where? She stood, wary of what was coming next. Rachel couldn't have possibly worked this fast. And the embassy was too far to have got a man up here already.

Whatever reservations she had, however,

she could do nothing but obey. She walked up to the bars and stuck her hands through. To her surprise, the guard shook his head and failed to produce handcuffs.

"*¿Dónde vamos?*" Where are we going? she asked as she followed him down the hall, looking ahead to see if Rafe was already waiting for her. Were they being released? It seemed too good to be true. Still, she preferred to be optimistic.

"Can I have my backpack now?" she said, pushing her luck.

But the man ignored her questions as he led her down the hallway. Some of the cages—to call them cells would have been an overstatement—were occupied by men, some by women. A number of the cages stood empty. She didn't see Rafe anywhere.

Then they were out in the filtered light of dusk at last. She took in the brown, worn-down Jeep ATV with POLICÍA painted on the side. It seemed to be waiting for her.

They were transferring her to someplace else. A few alarming options came to mind even as she tried not to jump to conclusions. The most likely explanation she could come up with was that they were taking her back to the army base. Maybe the military investigator couldn't come to Capunata for some reason, after all.

How long would they hold her there?

And again, where was Rafe?

She turned to the guard. *"¿Dónde es Señor Montoya?"*

But before the man could answer, Rafe came through the front door. Her heart gave a couple of slow thumps. He looked to be in a fierce mood but seemed to brighten when he saw her. He was under escort as well but unbound just like her. As soon as he reached her, he stepped forward to put himself between Isabelle and the men.

For once, the protective gesture—probably subconscious on his part—didn't bother her a bit. Relief flooded over her. She was no longer alone.

"Are you okay?" he asked, as he glanced back at her over his shoulder. "Did anyone hurt you?" He kept his sharp gaze on her face.

She shook her head. "I'm fine. You?" She searched his face for new bruises but couldn't find any.

He drew in a slow breath, let it out as his face relaxed. "Okay," he said. "Any idea what's going on?"

She shrugged just as one of the guards opened the back door of the car for them.

"Get in," he said, and closed the door once they were both in their seats.

Then he climbed in the front as the other one started up the engine. She looked out the window at the snowcapped mountain that towered above. Wherever they were going, at least they were going together. The thought gave her some measure of comfort.

"How was the questioning?" she asked.

"Brief," he said and wouldn't elaborate.

The small prison yard was behind them in seconds, then the gate lifted and they were out in the open, just a few hundred feet from the tree line. The Jeep ATV had regular locks. All they had to do was open the door, jump, then make a run for it. She gave Rafe a questioning look.

"Let's wait," he said under his breath. "If we can get out of this the right way, it'd be easier not to have the police and the army after us."

His words made sense but didn't make her

feel any better. Time was ticking. If they were in Miami, she would have had full faith in law enforcement. She knew little about the Laderan legal system, however. If the police held them much longer...

Everything came back to Sonya Botero. They didn't have time, because Sonya didn't have time.

Rafe reached for her hand, squeezed it and didn't let go. "I tried to bribe them to put us in the same cell." His lips stretched into a flat smile.

She didn't pull away. They still had to figure out what was going on between them, but not now. "Didn't have enough money?"

"Didn't have any money. They already had our backpacks."

She hadn't even thought about that—the backpacks with all their papers, their guns. They hadn't been put in the Jeep vehicle with them. "How are we going to get our equipment back?"

"Once our identities are confirmed and we're cleared and released, we should see the bags again. Don't expect to find everything, though."

She closed her eyes for a moment and just enjoyed the comfort of his nearness, his touch. She didn't care about what the guards would appropriate; their clothes could be easily replaced once they got their credit cards back, so could the guns. Rafe had got them off the street a couple of hours after their arrival in the country, while she'd been giving a press conference about the on-hold DeLeon-Botero wedding. Obviously, he had known where to look. As long as they had access to money they could buy anything. What they couldn't buy was time.

"I don't think we are being transferred to another prison," he said suddenly.

Something in the tone of his voice made her turn to look out the window and follow his gaze. To the left of them the road forked, one branch leading to a walled estate that lorded over its surroundings with substantial majesty. She drew up her eyebrows in surprise as the car turned toward it.

The stone walls seemed to go on forever on each side of the impressive wrought-iron gate that swung open silently at their arrival. What was this place? And once you were locked in, how did you get out?

Soon the house in the back became fully visible with its salmon-colored walls and arched doorways, the nine-foot-tall dark wood of the entry door that was carved with folk motifs. Some of the windows had wrought-iron security bars, repeating the same patterns, others had only shutters that stood wide open.

Rafe had been right—definitely not a prison. The place looked like a country estate for one of the rich and famous, a stark contrast to their previous accommodations.

She stared at the stunning front garden that led to the house, edged with exotic palm trees, the driveway curving around an elaborate fountain before coming to the hacienda's front steps.

Their car stopped and at the same moment the front door swung open, revealing a short, older man in a light linen suit.

Rafe narrowed his eyes as he watched him. "I don't like it," he said. "Who the hell is that?"

Chapter Five

Isabelle checked for security without being too obvious. No guards, at least none apparent at the moment. A few discreetly placed cameras were scattered high up on the walls. She turned her attention to the man who'd come down the steps and now headed toward them.

He looked to be in his fifties with graying hair that was impeccably combed and a pencil-thin mustache, walking with a purposeful stride without appearing to hurry.

"*Buenos Días, Señor y Señora. Soy Umberto.* My employer, Señor Alberto Martinez, would like the pleasure of your company as his guests while the matters with the authorities are resolved. If you allow me, I would be happy to escort you to your rooms. There is sufficient time to freshen up before dinner." His smile was impersonal, his accent flawless, his manner polite to a fault.

He dismissed the two policemen with a nod and gestured Isabelle and Rafe toward the entrance. "Please come in. And if you need anything at all, please don't hesitate to ask. I am at your service."

She looked at Rafe, and he gave her an imperceptible shrug. He didn't seem to have a better handle on the situation than she did.

Alberto Martinez.

The name sounded familiar, but Isabelle couldn't come up with a face to match it, nor could she remember where she'd heard it before. A relative of Juan DeLeon perhaps?

"Muchas gracias, Señor," Rafe said with an easy smile as they stepped inside.

"Muchas gracias," she repeated. Whoever their host was, the man had got them out of jail.

Umberto led them down a hallway that was as lavishly appointed as the outside of the house. She scanned the row of oil paintings in their gilded frames. The colors of the highly stylistic landscapes were dark, mostly black and gray with the occasional swirl of red, some kind of modern art she couldn't begin to understand. An art expert might have called them genius, but all she could think was cold and menacing.

Umberto stopped between the only two doors in the hallway, one on each side. "You can put your dirty laundry out in front of the door. It'll be taken care of. Dinner will be served in an hour. The dining room is in the middle of the house. Just go back the way we came and straight through the living room. I hope you will have a pleasant stay with us." He motioned Rafe to the room on the right and Isabelle to the room on the left, then gave another polite smile before he left them.

Curiosity drove her forward as she stepped into her room. She noticed the bottled water, the wine and the bowl of fruit first, went for an apple as she registered the antique furniture, the ornate copper chandelier, the two doors that she needed to investigate. Rafe came in before she reached the first one. He walked straight to the window.

"We should take this one," he said. "We can see the entrance from here. Keep track of who comes and goes." He looked her in the eye. "I'd rather not separate, if you don't mind."

He wanted to share her room.

The thought started some kind of chemical reaction in her body, with the side effect of pronounced tingling. She ignored it and hesitated only for a split second before nodding. Sticking together in a strange place seemed like a good idea. She glanced back at the large bed, wondered if his invitation extended to something more than shared work and decided to worry about that later.

"So who is our host? Do you know him?" she asked, as she pushed open the door she'd been heading for. Bathroom.

"Alberto Martinez. Big-time politician. Forgot to ask—did you get a chance to call Rachel?" Rafe walked around the perimeter of the room, checking the other door that was richly carved and looked a hundred years old.

"Yes. You called the embassy?" She stepped into the bathroom, and the muscles in her shoulders began to relax at the sight of the large claw-foot tub and thick cotton towels on the bench by the wall.

"Yes," he said behind her. "Maybe Rachel

talked to Juan. He and Martinez could be best friends for all I know. Juan could have asked him to help us."

Made sense. She drew a hand along the richly patterned antique tiles, looked at the gilded mirror that went from the floor to the ceiling behind the tub and caught sight of Rafe and the bed a few feet behind him. His dark gaze burned into hers, sending a jolt of awareness zinging through her body. God, she was pitiful. *Think business.* "So we're free?"

He waited a beat before he answered, and the look in his eyes said she wasn't fooling him a bit. "Not as good as that. My best guess is that we are under house arrest at Mr. Martinez's estate."

She nodded and turned around, passed by him, the spacious suite seeming too small all of a sudden. She walked toward the other door, which he had already opened while she'd been exploring the bathroom. It led to a magnificent veranda. Carved stone columns held up the arches, wrought-iron tables and chairs beckoned.

"Some house arrest." The contrast between

the filthy cell she'd occupied less than an hour ago and their current accommodations left her feeling lost and bewildered. "So where are our ankle bracelets?" she asked, as he stepped outside behind her.

"A guy like Alberto Martinez vouches for someone, it's good enough in this country." He smiled as he sat, stretching his long legs in front of him. "The butler said we had an hour to clean up. Why don't you go first."

She glanced at the smudges of dirt on her arm. "Thanks."

"Relax. Take your time. I have a feeling our reprieve won't be long-lived."

"Meaning?"

He shrugged. "Even if our troubles with the police are cleared up tomorrow, we'll have to rush to make up for time lost. And if nothing changes, we need to get out of here on our own."

Break out, he meant. She nodded and turned inside the room. On a lark, she checked the wooden armoire on her way to the bathroom. "Hey, there're clothes in here. You think I can take some?"

"Umberto said to put our dirty clothes by

the door. I think it's a safe bet they don't expect us to come to dinner naked," he called back from outside.

Her throat went dry at the picture of an intimate meal by candlelight, just the two of them, the only cloth in the room being under the plates.

Snap out of it.

She pulled a light but elegant dress that should be suitable for dinner, which, if the house was any indication, might be a fancy affair.

She turned on the water then went back to the living room while she waited for the tub to fill. Might as well call Rachel to give her an update. But oddly, a thorough search of the room did not turn up a phone.

"Are we too far out from the main drag to have phone lines?" she called out.

"I wouldn't think so," came the response from outside. "Not every house in Ladera has a phone in every room."

"I'll ask to use one when we meet our host at dinner."

She went back into the bathroom to check on the water. Ready. God, she couldn't wait to get clean. Her dirty clothes dropped to the tiles and she stepped into the tub, sank down to her neck, forgetting everything else for the moment except the blissful feeling of hot water enveloping her body.

She scrubbed her skin until it tingled, washed her hair, submerged under water for as long as her lungs allowed, to soak away the lingering remnants of jail. She felt a hundred percent better by the time she dried off and dressed.

Rafe opened one eye then the other, as she pulled on the dress, adjusting the spaghetti straps. The burnt-orange silk came to her knees. His gaze traveled her at length. He came to his feet grinning, stepped toward her but seemed to change his mind.

"Don't go anywhere until I come back, *querida.*" His voice was thick and suggestive.

Heat lapped at the V of her thighs.

Any thought that things would just go back to normal between them was nothing but a pipe dream. The realization left her angry and confused, angry that she'd put herself in this situation, confused because she was no longer sure what she really wanted. She looked after him as he disappeared behind the bathroom door, and after a minute or two her heartbeat returned to normal.

Something was happening between them.

Of course, this was certainly neither the place nor the time. She was in Ladera to save Sonya, not to worry about her own personal life.

Isabelle glanced around and walked across the veranda to investigate the house's immediate surroundings. Rafe was right. If Rachel and/or the embassy didn't come through, they might have to leave here in a hurry and, if at all possible, undetected. No better time than the present to get to know the lay of the land.

She strolled along the loose gravel that formed the winding pathways among palms and cacti, and inspected the hacienda, counting doors and windows on each level, noticing which had bars, which didn't.

When she heard voices from another one of the downstairs rooms whose windows stood open, she stopped to listen without hesitation.

ISABELLE RUSH. Her petite figure and that sweet southern smile she had inherited from her grandmother was an effective cover for the woman of steel and determination she was inside, just like her job of spokesperson at WYW was a cover for the tough confidential agent. She impressed him, intrigued him, challenged him on every level. She drove him crazy.

Rafe scrubbed the grime of the hillside and jail from his body, very much aware that just a few minutes ago it was her naked body in the same tub. He wanted her with an intensity that was disconcerting. He was a grown man, he had desired other women before. But not like this. She mattered.

He stood and shook water from his hair, spraying the terra-cotta tile floor, wishing away the very tangible proof that he'd been thinking about her in the tub. He should be thinking about Alberto Martinez and this new turn of events. Water ran down his body as he stepped out of the tub and towel-dried his limbs and torso, got as much water out of his hair as he could. How fast could Rachel get them out of here? And it would be Rachel who got the job done, although pressure from the embassy would help.

He stepped into the clothes that had been provided for him, a lightweight, high-quality suit of dark blue. He ran a finger over his freshly shaved chin, then combed through his hair. The first thing he saw when he stepped into the bedroom was Isabelle bending to fasten a high-heeled black sandal to her foot.

He drank in the sight of her for a few seconds. "You look beautiful."

Her gaze met his as she straightened. "You clean up pretty good yourself."

And he remembered that out on the veranda he'd been about to kiss her before he decided to be a gentleman and wash first. He'd delayed long enough. He walked over, turned the swivel chair she was sitting in so she would face him.

She tasted faintly of mint, the toothpaste they'd both used. He let himself get lost in her, in the feelings she brought. He grew harder, if that was possible. Then he became aware of something else, something odd—a pronounced feeling of relief. Relief that she was safe and in his arms. Relief that he had found her. It seemed insane. He hadn't been looking for her. He hadn't been looking for anyone.

And yet, an unbidden thought came from

some unexamined place: *This is it.* This was what he wanted—to go on kissing her for the rest of his life. Blood rushed in his ears as he pulled away, the idea leaving him dizzy.

Midlife crisis, he told himself, and with superhuman effort he forced a nonchalant smile as he offered her his arm, his heart beating against his chest as if it'd been taking kickboxing lessons. "Shall we go to dinner?"

A moment of confusion crossed her flushed face, then she turned back to the mirror and finger-combed her hair to repaired the damage he'd done. She knocked over a bottle of lotion as she stood, straightened it.

"Let's meet Martinez," she said, and avoided his eyes as she walked from the room.

The hallway was deserted.

"So I take it politics pays pretty good in this country," she remarked casually.

How on earth could she make her brain switch gears this fast? His was still on the kiss, but he managed to focus it on her question. "Not the office itself, but the bribes, yes." He gave her a rueful smile. "But Martinez came from money anyway. His family owns a couple of important mines."

And the wealth was displayed everywhere he looked—the oil paintings that lined the walls, the furniture, the Inca artifacts and statuettes that could easily compete with the collection of any museum.

They reached the end of the hall and turned toward the middle of the house, walking across the foyer. Martinez was already in the living room, looking suave in his expensive suit. He was in his mid-sixties, his hair more silver than black, his body kept in excellent shape. As they stepped into the room, he set aside the folder of documents he'd been reading and stood, moving with ease and elegance.

"Bienvenidos. Welcome." He came over, kissed Isabelle's hand before shaking Rafe's. "I am so pleased that you could join me. When I heard Juan's friends met with some unpleasantness, I had to see if I could help."

"We appreciate it, Señor Martinez." Rafe measured up the man. "So you talked to Juan recently?"

The man's smile widened, revealing the best dentures money could buy. "I wish I could. He hasn't been back in his offices for some time. I understand he's still in Miami, yes? Unfortunate tragedy, his fiancée. And after what happened to his wife." The man shook his head, his face softening into a look of sympathy. "No man should have to bear so much heartache."

"Hopefully, Sonya will be returned soon," Isabelle said.

"*Naturalmente.*" Martinez stepped back and gestured them toward the leather armchairs that formed a circle around a low table. "Please, make yourselves comfortable. May I offer you a drink?"

"Thank you."

They both accepted the wine, the same brand that had been thoughtfully provided in their room.

"My own," Martinez said with pride. "I have a small vineyard. Not enough for commercial bottling and full-scale production, but the family likes it and the vines produce enough for us."

"It's excellent," Isabelle remarked politely.

"Thank you, *señora.*" Martinez flashed her a smile that brimmed with appreciation. "Sometimes I fantasize about expanding and spending more time with my grapes. Maybe after retirement."

A retirement that could come sooner rather than later if Juan's bill of limiting political terms came to pass into law, Rafe thought, and wondered how Martinez felt about Juan DeLeon's political agenda.

Isabelle leaned forward. "Would you mind if I used your phone, Señor Martinez?"

"No, of course not. The house phones are still out of service, unfortunately. We had some hard winds a few days ago. Let me give you my cell phone." He patted his right jacket pocket then the other one. "I'm sorry. Must have left it upstairs in the office. I'll have someone bring it down." He lifted his glass from the table as he rose. "Why don't we get started on dinner? I'd love to hear how my good friend Juan is doing and, of course, about the terrible misunderstanding you had in town. An outrage. You must forgive our police. The army is putting a lot of pressure on them right now."

He led the way through an arched doorway into a courtyard that was open to the dark sky above, a Spanish fountain gurgling gently in the middle, giant potted palms lining the walls. Another arched doorway directly across led into the dining room, where massive dark wood chairs and a table set for dinner waited for them.

"Please, allow me." Martinez pulled out Isabelle's seat for her with old-fashioned flourish, just as Rafe was about to catch up and do the same.

"Thank you." Isabelle smiled sweetly, her fawn-colored eyes sweeping the room, the dozens of candles and antique china. "It's beautiful," she said, her appreciation for the setting showing in her voice.

"Nothing here could be compared to the beauty of our present company." Martinez's face was stretched into a permanent smile as he sat next to her.

Rafe watched them from the corner of his eye. He liked the guy less and less with each passing moment.

"Enjoy your meal," their host said, as a servant brought in the first course, a spicy local soup.

Rafe shoveled in a spoonful, distracted by the way Martinez was looking at Isabelle, then paused. *Diosmío,* a warm meal felt good going down. The familiar spices were awakening his tongue, his senses.

"So my friend, DeLeon, is doing well and staying in *los Estados Unidos?*" Martinez asked.

"Yes, for now he'll stay in Miami," Isabelle replied, starting on the agreed-upon story. "His soon-to-be father-in-law is unwell and needs his support. They're hoping to hear again from the kidnappers. As long as Sonya is in the U.S., Juan will remain there also."

The plan was to not let anyone know they had information on Sonya's having been moved out of the country. They wanted to take the kidnappers by surprise.

"Mmm." Martinez nodded.

Rafe watched him closely. He could swear he saw a flash of relief crossing his face before he schooled it back to his previous look of concern and compassion.

"And you work with Juan on his wedding?" Martinez asked, this time looking directly at Rafe.

If he hoped to rile him by mocking him for working for a wedding planner, he wouldn't achieve his purpose. Rafe liked his cover. It often caused his enemies to underestimate him, an advantage he used to achieve success in his missions.

"We both work for Weddings Your Way, the company that's organizing Señor DeLeon's wedding," he said. "Isabelle is our spokesperson, and I work in security. The director of our company thought it would be best to send us to talk with Juan's family and reassure them, and also make a statement to the Laderan media. A wedding as high-profile as this…" He shrugged lightly. "There is a lot of interest, a lot of speculation."

"Yes, of course. Juan is a public figure. A wonderful man—he's done a lot for our country." Martinez leaned back in his chair, allowing the servant to take his soup bowl.

Rafe did the same, trying to guess how many people he employed at this country estate. "Do you come here often?"

"As often as work allows." He smiled as the next course arrived, the giant slices of steak still sizzling.

Rafe helped himself, adding some grilled peppers to his plate, glad for Isabelle's sake that they weren't in the south of the country where instead of beef the meat served would have been more likely goat.

Laderan diet largely consisted of different meats. He hadn't forgotten, but over the years he'd become used to the foods of Miami, the variety that came from Cuba, Mexico and the Korean and Chinese immigrants.

And as he savored the beef it occurred to him that if he had a house instead of a third-floor condo, he could have a traditional Laderan cookout from time to time and invite some friends from work. Like Isabelle. What did she do with her free time? They should hang out more. They were both alone.

Alone.

Odd that he would think of it like that suddenly. He'd always classified himself as happily single.

He watched Martinez and Isabelle chat about the pictures on the wall. Apparently, they depicted Señora Martinez, who'd passed on a few years ago, and their five wonderful children—two boys and three girls. For some reason, this gallery of "happy family" photos made him feel more morose by the minute.

It seemed Isabelle was right after all. Being

back in Ladera *was* pushing him into a midlife crisis. Coming back had always held mixed emotions for him, but this time somehow he felt everything intensified. It would pass when he went back to Miami, he told himself. He wasn't going to give up his perfectly good condo for some house that would take up all his free time with never-ending repairs. He'd get a convertible maybe. That was what men did with their midlife crisis, wasn't it?

A convertible and a scorching affair. He watched Isabelle, smiling and animated, looking breathtaking in the candlelight. *Scorching* didn't begin to cover it. Of course, she was regretting their night at the temple already. And, unfortunately, she was the only woman he wanted.

The thought was so wrong on so many levels, he shut it down as soon as it surfaced and joined in the conversation that had moved on to the estate's history.

After dinner, flan was served and ice cream—*dulce de leche,* a sweet caramel flavor. Coffee came after that, then, once they moved out to the veranda, the servants brought *pisco*.

"Brandy," he explained to Isabelle as she swirled the amber liquid in her glass.

He watched her slim fingers, the slow sensuous movement of her arms, and took a bigger than intended gulp of his own drink.

"Made from my own grapes," Martinez said proudly, and turned the topic of conversation to small talk about his vineyard in the south. "But you must be tired," he said, after no more than thirty minutes. "I shouldn't keep you from your rest. We'll have many days to enjoy each other's company."

Enjoy was a strong word, but the meeting had definitely been interesting, Rafe thought as he stood.

"The phone?" Isabelle asked.

"Yes, yes. Sorry, I've forgotten. It's rare that I have such interesting guests out here. I'll have a cell phone sent to your room. Feel free to keep it while you are here. I'm sure you are both anxious to talk to your family and friends. Speaking of family," he said to Rafe, "is yours from around here?"

"To the south."

"Anyone I might know?"

"I don't think so. They're not in the public

eye as you are. Thank you for your hospitality." Rafe nodded to the man and deliberately reached for Isabelle's hand, not having liked the way Martinez had looked at her through the evening.

"*Buenas noches.*" Their host was all smiles.

"And a good night to you." And deep sleep, he thought as he walked down the hall with Isabelle at his side. Deep sleep and captivating dreams because he hadn't bought any of Martinez's smarmy hospitality. He had every intention of searching the estate tonight.

"ARE YOU CRAZY?" Isabelle took off her sandals, which were a half size too small but bearable. The clothing in the armoire belonged to Martinez's daughter, he'd told her over dinner. She always left some clothes at the estate in case she ever decided to stop in on a spontaneous visit. He assured her she wouldn't mind lending a few pieces to a guest in need.

"If somebody catches us snooping and our host throws us out, we are going back to jail," she reminded Rafe.

"He's not going to catch me. Besides, you snooped around earlier."

"I took a walk in the garden and checked out possible points of exit in case the police take too long to clear us. I didn't go into any rooms or through our host's personal stuff."

"You listened to his personal conversation from under a window."

"Well, maybe I shouldn't have. In any case, he didn't say anything remotely suspicious. I told you. He is just expecting another guest, that's all."

"I don't like Martinez."

There was a finality in Rafe's voice that she thought was a tad too stubborn. "He seems like a perfect gentleman to me."

Okay, that wasn't completely true. He seemed like he tried hard to appear to be a perfect gentleman. He'd also at times appeared evasive and forced in his joviality, but she pretty much figured it came with the fact that he was a politician.

Rafe was standing by the window, looking out. "Why is he at his country estate during the height of political arguments at the capital? The House is in session and there are a couple of bills up for vote that are the most hotly contested ones in recent history."

The question stopped her for a moment. Juan had mentioned a couple of times how crucial these weeks were. Which is why Rafe thought that a political opponent of his might have been involved in the kidnapping, to keep Juan occupied and out of the country for a while.

She was convinced Maggie, Juan's ex-wife, was involved somehow. Her doctor, Dr. Ramon, had tried to kill Sonya Botero's limo driver in the U.S., then committed suicide once Miami Confidential took him into custody. Maggie's cousin, Jose Fuentes, was caught at the last aborted ransom handover attempt. The ex-wife was in this, in the thick of it. Maybe the kidnapping was motivated by jealousy.

Or maybe, by drugs. Some of Maggie's family meddled in the drug trade. One of them could have met up with Dr. Ramon during a visit. One of Juan's bills would have delivered a serious strike to the drug trade if passed into law.

Which brought her back to thinking how important this week was for those bills, for everyone in politics in Ladera. So why wasn't Martinez at work?

"Maybe he had an emergency here?" she suggested.

"Like what?" Rafe slid down in his armchair and put his feet up on a small leather ottoman.

"Problems with whatever he grows here."

"It's not a working ranch. It's his gentleman's estate. His vineyards are in the south. Why is he sitting in the middle of nowhere when a fierce political fight is going on in the capital?"

"I don't know. But he says he's a friend of Juan."

"He says," Rafe repeated.

"He's been nice to us. We'd still be sitting in jail without him. If he's one of Juan's enemies, why would he be helping us?"

"Is he really helping? Or did he want to keep a closer eye on us? Where is the phone?"

More than an hour had passed since they'd retired after dinner, but nobody had shown up with the promised cell phone yet.

She shrugged. "Maybe the servants are busy cleaning up."

"Or maybe he doesn't want us to talk to anyone."

She knew Rafe's instincts had been dead-on too many times to dismiss his concerns now, and she was suddenly uneasy. "Maybe we should take a quick look at the house. I suppose it wouldn't hurt to find out what he's really about."

He unfolded his long legs and stood. "At the very least, we need to find a phone. We should let Rachel know where we are. And I wouldn't mind coming across a small handgun or two. Hate going around in a strange place unarmed."

"I don't think we need to worry about him. He's slick. He's a politician, it comes with the territory. But I didn't get any killer vibes from him. Murder takes a different kind of man."

"I'll take your word for it," he said with a slight nod. "You're the criminologist." But then the easy smile slipped off his face and when he stepped closer and reached for her hand, the expression he wore was so intense she felt the heat of it. "Be careful and stick close to me."

She swallowed. "I'm always careful. But I go wherever necessary to get the job done."

He watched her for a moment before he responded. "That's exactly the kind of talk that makes me crazy about you," he said, then he leaned in and brushed his lips over hers, lingered.

Her throat went dry again. *No, no, no.* She glanced away from his burning gaze, but her eyes went straight to the bed two steps behind Rafe. *Can't happen.* This was not why they were here. They had a job to do.

"You can only put me off for so long, Isabelle," he warned her as he moved back a little. "I fully intend to explore what is going on between us."

"Nothing," she said, and watched as his face turned serious.

"You don't lie. It's one of the things I like about you. You shouldn't start now, not about this, not to yourself." He was still holding her hands.

"Okay. There is something," she said. After all, wasn't acknowledgement of the problem the first step toward recovery?

"See how easy the truth is?" His dark eyes

swirled with heat. "Now keep going with it. Say, *Rafe, I want you to kiss me,*" he said, his voice thick, and pulled her closer.

God help her, she did want him. "We should go," she said but couldn't look away from his eyes.

"Plenty of time. We have to wait until the whole house is asleep."

"Rafe, I—"

He seemed too impatient to find out whether she would admit what she wanted or come up with another excuse, and she wasn't sure herself how she would have finished the sentence had he not kissed her.

Nobody on this earth could kiss like Rafe Montoya.

His lips were...perfect, she thought in a haze of pleasure—not too soft, not too hard, not too small, not too big. She was turning into Goldilocks.

So what if his lips were perfect? The rest of their crazy attraction was not. They were bad, bad, bad for each other.

He pulled away and searched her face. "You're thinking."

Not enough, apparently, because she kept

ending up in his arms. What could she possibly say in a situation like this?

She cleared her throat. "Okay. I'm attracted to you. But I don't want whatever is between us to go any further than it already has."

"Why?"

"Because we can't possibly have a future together. We don't want the same things, Rafe. You know it."

"You know what I want?"

"I can guess," she said drily, and glanced toward his hardness still pressed against her.

"I want other things, too. You'd be surprised. I—"

The sound of a car arriving stopped the conversation. But, by the time they rushed to the window, the car had pulled out of their range of vision, blocked by the greenery of the garden.

She grabbed his hand and pulled him out to the veranda. If anyone saw them, it would look like they were out for a late-night stroll.

"This way." She crossed the garden.

His long fingers closed around hers as they walked without seeming to hurry, her body still buzzing from his kiss, her brain trying to digest the conversation that had followed.

He stopped at the edge of the row of palms, and she slowly refocused. A black Mercedes sedan parked by the front steps. They were only able to catch a glimpse of the driver before he entered the house. He was about the same age as their host, but much worse dressed, middle height, Hispanic.

"You know him?" Isabelle asked.

Rafe shook his head. "I suppose we'll find out who he is in the morning." He continued down the path, walking slowly, still hanging on to her.

A window closed on an upper floor somewhere, but by the time Isabelle looked up she could only see a disappearing shadow. "Probably just a maid."

"We should stay out here for a few more minutes," he said.

She scanned the few windows that were still lit and the ones that were dark, not too comfortable with the thought that someone might be spying on them from a darkened room. She wanted to believe that Martinez was who he made himself out to be, that they'd be out of here tomorrow and find Sonya. She wanted to believe that this thing she was feeling for Rafe would resolve itself without her losing her heart in the process.

A gust of wind swooped down and twirled a few blades of dry grass around her shoes. She shivered.

"Cold?" Rafe let go of her hand and draped an arm around her. "We can go back in, if you'd like."

"No, it's fine," she said. If someone was watching them, they had to play out their lovers' stroll in the garden. If Martinez was having them watched, he would know by now that they were sharing a room.

She walked along beside Rafe and soaked up the heat of his body. The stars were brilliant, the air crisp, the hacienda beautiful enough to be painted.

Protesting never even crossed her mind when he stopped and pulled her closer. There was nothing tentative about his kiss, nothing superficial. He kissed her as a man kisses a woman who belongs to him.

And all of a sudden she felt as if they'd kissed hundreds of times like this before, and the promise of the next hundred, the next thousand, was in every small sound they made, in the way they could not get enough of each other, in the slow stirring sensation in the middle of her chest that grew into a sweet ache under the starlit sky.

Chapter Six

Midnight passed before the house quieted down and they could finally get started on their clandestine mission. They were back in their own clothes, which had been laundered and ironed and returned to their room by the time they had finished dinner.

"This way," Rafe whispered, as they reached the end of the hallway and had to choose whether to go upstairs or to the front of the house, where the public rooms—living room, dining room and courtyard—were.

He chose the downstairs rooms. They'd seen those before. That familiarity and the moonlight that filtered in the windows should help them navigate in the dark and avoid bumping into furniture.

He moved forward but stopped again as he

heard a small noise from upstairs. He tensed as the sound came again.

"Somebody's snoring," Isabelle whispered behind him.

After a moment, he realized she was right and he moved on.

His gaze settled on the poker next to the living room fireplace. Not a bad weapon, but, should they get caught, how would he explain it? The plan was, if they woke anyone, Isabelle would say she was having stomach cramps and Rafe was escorting her to find a servant to ask for some medicine. The poker did not fit into that cover.

He saw moonlight glinting off a letter opener on a desk and picked it up, handed it to Isabelle. The piece of sharp metal wasn't much, but it was small enough to be concealed, which she did immediately.

He riffled through the papers on top of the desk while she searched the two shallow drawers. Newspaper clippings and stock reports—nothing exciting, nothing he could remotely connect to Juan DeLeon or Sonya Botero.

He moved on, looked over the bookshelf,

lifted up a few volumes to see if there might be some documents hidden behind them, but came up empty. He nearly upset the phone table as he turned, knocking off the receiver but catching it a few inches above the tile floor.

He paused at the buzz that indicated an open line, lifted the receiver to his ear. "It works."

Had Martinez lied or had the lines been repaired since dinner?

The maid had never shown up with the promised cell phone. He dialed Rachel's number while considering the situation.

"Rachel, it is Rafe. Listen, we're at Alberto Martinez's estate under house arrest. What can you find out about the guy?" he whispered, once she picked up on the other end.

"Hang on a sec," she said.

A couple of minutes passed before she got back on the line, time he spent watching Isabelle search through the room.

"Used to be one of Juan's allies, now Martinez is one of his biggest enemies. He stands to lose millions if Juan's bills pass."

"Thanks, Rachel."

"He's been linked to some undesirable elements. Watch out and keep safe. Things are in motion. I might be able to get you out of there by midmorning."

He thanked her again and hung up, went to help Isabelle as she moved on to the next room. The courtyard took only a minute or two—nothing there but plants. They had to be careful; four windows on the second floor faced the courtyard. All were dark, but that didn't necessarily mean that no one was awake behind them. They moved on to the dining room, but the china cabinets hadn't yielded any secrets, either. Another hallway opened beyond that with three doors—bathroom, kitchen, pantry. They went through those fast as well. It seemed theirs were the only guestrooms on the first floor. The new visitor who'd arrived after dinner had to be staying upstairs.

"Where do the servants live?" Isabelle whispered, as she closed the kitchen door behind her, careful not to make a sound.

"Probably in one of the smaller buildings in the back."

An arrangement that suited him because this way they didn't have to worry about a maid waking in the middle of the night and discovering their clandestine search mission.

"Upstairs?" he mouthed the word and glanced toward the curving staircase.

She nodded and went first, placing her footsteps with care until she ensured the stairs weren't creaking. He followed her up, using just as much caution. They had to be more careful now. There were people up here—Martinez and the guest, to start with. Most likely, there was at least one personal servant, too, tucked somewhere in the back, in case the lord of the house needed something in the middle of the night. And Rafe was sure Martinez would have his security goons up there with him, too. He'd caught glimpses of two men during their walk in the garden. Apparently, Martinez felt he needed protection even on his own estate but wasn't concerned enough to have them keep night watch.

The upstairs hallway was clear.

"Which way?" she mouthed.

Two corridors curved in front of them, one to the left, one to the right.

His instincts said to stick together so he could keep an eye on her, protect her if necessary. But he also knew that she was more than capable of protecting herself. And if they stayed together, they'd hinder each other rather than be of help, couldn't tell if a noise was made by the other or someone else sneaking up on them.

"I take this wing, you take that one," he said and waited. If she showed the slightest hesitation, he'd go with her.

But she took off without a second glance at him.

He stood there another moment, looked after her as she stole down the hall, watched her move with practiced ease. Then he went to see what he could find out about Martinez in the wing he'd chosen to cover.

Luck was with him: the first door he opened led to a study. The room was spacious, leather and antique wood everywhere, their scent mingling with that of cigar smoke. Moonlight glinted off the glass from rows of pictures on the wall—Martinez with famous people and other celebrities.

Rafe moved to the desk and looked through the paperwork, finding little more than general correspondence, letters of congratulations and thank-yous. He glanced around the room for a computer but didn't find one. He would have loved to have seen the more informal e-mails Martinez sent to his friends. Maybe the man had taken his laptop with him to the bedroom.

He rifted through stock reports and quarterly statements from the Martinez mines. The figures, combined with those they'd seen earlier downstairs, made one thing perfectly clear: Martinez was losing money. Big-time.

Rafe searched for an appointment book, but that, too, was missing. Could be that Ramirez kept an electronic calendar on his laptop. He would have to get his hands on that somehow. Ramirez was acting odd all around. He was one of Juan's enemies, pretending to others to be his friend. The whole phone's-out-of-service thing was fishy, especially since they'd just made a call. He was trying to keep Rafe and Isabelle isolated. But for what purpose?

Rafe left the study and crept down the hall, figured the bedroom wouldn't be too far from the study. He needed to get in there and root out what secrets Ramirez was hiding.

THE FIRST DOOR Isabelle eased open led to an empty guest room, looking very much the same as the one Rafe and she occupied down-stairs—spacious and elegantly furnished with antiques. The second room stood empty as well. Another guest room, she figured from the lack of personal clutter that tended to accumulate in a person's bedroom. Not that this room was completely empty. Someone had been in there recently. Clothes were draped over the back of a chair, the blankets rumpled as if someone had briefly lain on top of them.

The new guest.

She glanced toward the open bathroom door—dark, no movement.

Midnight had passed. Where was the guy? What business did he have outside of his room while everybody slept?

Isabelle stepped inside and closed the door behind her without making a sound.

She moved over to the foot of the bed and opened the small suitcase that leaned against it. She found it empty—not even a change of clothes. Strange.

Next, she searched the discarded suit hanging on the back of the chair, ran her fingers through the pockets. Nothing there, either. Wait. She felt something hard and picked up the jacket to see what it was and where. And then she saw it: an empty gun holster, not in the jacket after all, but under it, under his folded pants.

Whoever the man was, he was armed.

Her fingers skimmed to the letter opener tucked into the waistband of her pants. Not much defense against a hail of bullets. And Rafe had even less. She hurried to the door silently and eased it open. She had to get to Rafe to warn him. But before she could step out into the hallway, the thick wood of the door was shoved back in her face, and the man whose room she'd just searched pushed his way in, his gun leveled at her head.

"¿Qué estás haciendo aquí?" What are you doing here?

"Lo siento. Estoy perdida. I'm lost. I was looking for a maid or someone to help. I'm a guest here. *Soy una huésped aquí."*

He moved forward, forcing her to step back until she was in the middle of the room. "Turn around."

She hesitated. As soon as she turned, he would see the letter opener at her back. It'd be hard to explain. No way out of this but fighting. Unlike Martinez, this man did have murder in his eyes. In a split-second decision she went for the thin blade of metal, aiming for the man's throat with her right hand while pushing up the gun with her left.

She hit flesh but not the right spot and not deep enough. The butt of the handgun slammed against her temple, making her lose her balance for a second as she stumbled. He took advantage of the temporary weakness and shoved her onto the bed on her stomach. Her hands were tied behind her back the next second.

She was breathing hard, her face pressed into the bedclothes. There had to be a way out of this. Could she roll off the bed and kick his feet from under him? If he dropped the gun... She shifted, wanting to get a look at exactly where he was standing now.

Too close.

And came closer still, bending over her. "Do something as stupid as that again, *bruja,* and you won't live to regret it," he said next to her ear and flipped her, shoved something into her mouth before she could respond.

She gagged from the handful of cloth that

pressed down on her tongue and stuck to the roof of her mouth, silencing her effectively. She kicked at him, but he stepped aside easily then he yanked her to standing, one hand on her arm, the other holding the gun to her back.

"Don't make any noise," he said, and forced her to walk across the room in front of him.

She hoped to see Rafe in the hallway, but all was quiet and empty outside the room.

Where was he?

She had to get his attention somehow. She glanced at the stairs. Did she dare throw herself down to make some noise? What if Ramirez and his goons woke? Would they be on the attacker's side? He was, after all, a guest of Ramirez. What the hell did the man want, anyway?

Isabelle shuffled forward as slowly as she dared, keeping her eyes on the shadows. Then she was at the top of the stairs and hesitated for a moment. God, they looked steep. If she made herself tumble and hurt herself too badly... Not a good idea. She needed to be whole and ready to fight when Rafe finally caught up with them.

Their footsteps on the stairs weren't loud

enough to wake someone from a sound sleep, but Rafe, who would be listening for sounds, should catch it. They were halfway down now. Why hadn't he heard them yet? Had the attacker got to him already?

The thought filled her chest with cold pain and she stumbled, but the man caught her from behind, held her tighter. He took her toward the back of the house, across the kitchen and through the servants' door in the back.

The night air hit her, sending a shiver skittering across her skin. He shoved her forward, gravel crunching beneath their shoes. Where were they going? Then she spotted the small building in the back of the garden, an empty storage shed she had checked out earlier that afternoon.

And suddenly, without a shadow of a doubt, she knew he was taking her there to kill her.

SONYA LAY IN THE DIRT, struggling with despair. She didn't have long. She was weak from hunger, scared at the change in her captors that was becoming more and more apparent as the days went by and they moved her around, traveling miles each night.

They were getting tired of her, getting tired of their assignment. They were sloppier now, too, watching her less closely, and it added to her frustration to know that she was long past the point when she could have taken advantage of it.

She watched them as they sat around, having finished dinner. Her stomach growled at the sight of the collection of small bones on the ground. Sometimes they still let her have the scraps.

One of the men brought a bucket of water, the others dipped their cups into it to drink. When they were done, a few washed their faces and hands in what remained. The largest of the men, Pisco, nicknamed after his favorite drink, caught her watching and their gaze met for a moment before she hastily looked away.

Too late.

She could see from the corner of her eye as he stood. She curled up in a tight ball in defense, hardly able to believe it when he picked up the bucket and brought it with him.

"Agua?" He stopped a few feet from her.

"Sí, Señor. Por favor," she begged.

He lifted the bucket higher and tossed the water into her face.

Tears sprang to her eyes, blended into the drops of water on her face. *Don't give up. You can't give up.* She reached out her tongue and licked the water from around her lips, then she spotted a cupful or so that had gathered in an indentation in the ground next to her head, and she leaned forward and drank it, ignoring the taste of mud and the mocking laughter of the men.

RAFE FOLLOWED THE PAIR in the shadows, his movements cool and calculating, betraying nothing of the rage he felt inside. The bastard had his hands on Isabelle.

Palm trees swayed in the wind above, their leaves rubbing together in a swooshing sound, covering his footfall. He needed a weapon. He had hoped he would find one inside, but there had been none in Martinez's study, and before he could have searched the bedroom he had heard sounds at the other end of the hall and had gone to investigate.

Who was Martinez's guest?

Didn't matter. He would know soon enough when he searched the body for ID.

He watched Isabelle's slow progress. Was she hurt or was she just trying to gain some time? He looked her over carefully, couldn't see any obvious injury nor any darker patches on her clothes that might indicate blood, but they were at least a hundred yards ahead of him.

At last, they reached the low, brick shed and the man shoved Isabelle inside then closed the door behind them.

Rafe stepped out from behind the bush that had lent him cover and made a dash for the building, moving as fast as he could while staying in a crouch. He would not allow himself to think what the man planned to do with her, kept his full attention on each step he took, making sure he didn't make any noise that would alert the bastard to his rapidly approaching demise.

The shed had only one window—most of its glass missing. Rafe went to it and peeked inside. He saw nothing but darkness for the few seconds before his eyes adjusted.

"What are you doing in Ladera?" he heard

the man ask in Spanish. Finally, he could see a figure standing in the middle of the room, his gun still in hand but no longer pointed at Isabelle. He probably figured he had her under control.

"I'm here to handle a few press conferences. Who are you?" she asked, her back straight. If she was scared, she didn't show it.

"What were you doing in my room?"

"I got lost. I told you. I was looking for the maid. Look, there's no need for this, I—"

"Did Juan DeLeon send you here?"

"To Ladera? My supervisor at Weddings Your Way sent us here to handle publicity. But, of course, we are here on Señor DeLeon's behalf as well. He is our client. I don't understand what this is about." She was doing a good job at sounding exasperated and clueless.

"What is the bastard planning now?" The man's voice became more heated, apparently not buying the act despite Isabelle's best efforts.

"I'm not sure what you mean. Listen, it's all a misunderstanding—"

The rest of what she was going to say was cut off when the man slapped her with the back of his hand.

Rage washed through Rafe, cold and hard. Weapon or no weapon, the next second he grabbed on to the roof and pulled his body up, kicked in the window frame. Before the man knew what was happening, they were rolling on the ground, over the broken glass.

The bastard was doing his best to bring his gun up. Hell no. Rafe smashed the guy's hand into the ground, then caught sight of Isabelle moving closer, intent on helping.

"Get back!" he yelled at her, unable to gain control of the weapon, very much aware that it could go off blindly.

Come on, come on, come on. He threw his whole weight into the fight and finally pinned the man's wrist to the floor, squeezed hard, trying to snap the bone to force him to drop the gun.

He almost succeeded but hadn't counted on the knife. The bastard brought the switchblade out of nowhere. It nicked Rafe on the cheek before he gained control of that hand, too, rolling again, crunching more broken glass, locked in a desperate battle.

Then, he was finally able to maneuver the fight over to the corner beam and lifted his body, locked tightly with the other man's, heaved hard to slam the man's head against the beam. He went limp just long enough for Rafe to get the weapons away from him, tossing the knife to Isabelle, keeping the gun for himself and aiming it between the bastard's eyes as he pulled him up to standing.

"Who are you?"

The guy spit, red, but missed him.

"I'm in a pisser of a bad mood, amigo. I'm not going to ask you again."

The man's eyes boiled with hate. He kept his mouth shut. He'd hurt Isabelle. Thinking beyond that seemed increasingly hard. Rafe moved the gun lower, inch by inch, until the barrel pushed against the fly of the man's pants.

"Rafe?" Isabelle called, with that should-you-be-doing-this tone in her voice and stepped closer. A mistake on her part if she meant to bring him back to reasonable because, now that she was in his field of vision, he could see the red mark on her face where the bastard had hit her.

"Stay back," he said, then turned his attention to the man in front of him again. "Talk."

Son of a bitch wasn't going to play with him, damn it.

The bastard would have killed Isabelle. The thought made his blood run cold even as rage still pumped through him. The man had had his hands on her. Had hit her. It seemed extremely difficult at the moment to think beyond that. Rafe's fingers tightened on the gun.

The man had the gall to give him a snarly smile. "You don't have the balls." He spit the words in Spanish.

Oh, no? Go to hell, then, Rafe thought, and pulled the trigger.

Nothing happened, but the air seemed to have frozen around them. For a moment, nobody moved.

"Misfire," he said, a little stunned, into the guy's face, which had gone white. "Do you think it will happen again?" He shoved the gun another inch forward and noticed the beading sweat on the man's forehead.

"Rodrigo." The single word came out with a hoarse sound. "San…" All of a sudden, he didn't seem able to finish.

"Rodrigo Santiago." Rafe completed the name for him as pieces of the puzzle fell into place. Rodrigo Santiago, one of Juan's worst enemies, whom everyone had thought dead for years until recently when Miami Confidential came across some clues that Rodrigo might be still alive.

"Where is Sonya?" Rafe asked, about two inches from the man's face. He was done playing.

"No Sonya," he said, his voice holding none of his earlier bravado.

"I don't believe it. What are you doing here? Coming after us? You hate Juan. He ruined your life. I'm betting you hate him enough to cause him as much misery as you can."

"*Sí.*" The man's eyes hardened again at the mention of Juan's name, and he seemed to draw some strength from the hate he carried for his old enemy. "I hate him enough to kill him. And I'm man enough to do that. I don't need to play games with his woman."

I hate him enough to kill him.

A few pieces of the puzzle fell into place. "You were behind the assassination attempt in Ladera?"

"I *was* the assassin," he said with contempt. "I want to be there when the dog dies. God was not with me that day. I had done bad things. But I atoned. Now he is with me and he will give me my enemy."

He seemed too far gone on revenge for Rafe to explain that to assassinate anyone would be considered along with the other "bad things" as far as God was concerned.

"So you want to take out Juan DeLeon. Why come after us?"

"I know he sent you for me. I hear two people with guns were caught in Capunata, my town. I hear you work for DeLeon. He found out where I was. Perhaps he sent you to kill me. I had to kill you first."

Rafe shook his head, but didn't bother explaining. Just as well that they'd run into the man. He seemed to hate DeLeon with a fanaticism that would not have let him quit until he reached his goal.

"We have to call the police," Isabelle said.

He took a deep breath and nodded, kept the gun on the man while undoing the tie Isabelle had been bound with. She helped him by tying up Rodrigo.

Then he shoved the man into the corner and turned him toward the wall, keeping the weapon aimed at him with one hand as he pulled Isabelle closer with the other. For a long moment, he looked her over. "Are you hurt?"

She shook her head.

He tightened his hold on her and pressed his lips to hers, tight and hard—their circumstances didn't allow for more. Didn't allow for anything, really, but he needed to feel that she was all right, there and whole in his arms.

"We should go back to the house and call the police," she said when he let her go, her eyes all soft and tawny.

He nodded, his thoughts finding their way back to the task at hand. "I'd love to hear what our host has to say about this."

Chapter Seven

Alberto Martinez looking genuinely bewildered after having woken up from a sound sleep, claimed to know his guest as Antonio Waldez, a small-time businessman. His security flanked him as he sat in his leather armchair in the living room, glancing from Rodrigo to Rafe and back.

From time to time, his gaze skimmed the gun tucked into Rafe's belt. It made him nervous, Isabelle thought, but that alone couldn't be construed as anything suspicious. They couldn't expect him to jump for joy at having an armed man in his house who was questioning him in regard to an assassination attempt and a kidnapping.

"Look, I help people if it is in my power to do so, and often it is. Señor Waldez came to me to ask for a small loan. I promised I would consider it carefully and take a day or two to talk his proposition over with him."

Rodrigo was looking at the floor. He had not said a word since Rafe had dragged him into the house.

"Same with you," Martinez went on. "I heard that friends of a friend are in trouble and I opened my home. You could have turned out to be bad people. You could have turned out to be the ones who put that bomb by the base. Should I withhold help because there is some small chance I'll be taken advantage of? I don't think so. That's not the man I am, not the kind of life I want to live."

The words were right, but still, something about them reminded Isabelle of a practiced campaign speech. "And you called the police?" She lifted an eyebrow.

"*Sí, señorita*. They should be here within minutes. I don't tolerate violence in my house. I'm terribly sorry you were attacked here. I hope that's not how you will remember me and Ladera."

She nodded in acceptance of his apology and glanced at Rafe who seemed thoughtful.

Rodrigo had sworn he had nothing to do

with Sonya's kidnapping, and she was inclined to believe him. He had, after all, confessed to the assassination attempt on Juan. He was caught and knew he was going to jail either way. But he seemed in earnest when questioned about Juan's fiancée, his words, tone of voice and body language giving no sign of deception.

Same with Martinez. Isabelle was skeptical about the man's claims that he hadn't known Rodrigo's true identity, but when the discussion came to Sonya she didn't think he was hiding anything.

"You must believe me, *señorita*. This is terrible for me as well. News of this will be all over the media. Rodrigo Santiago found alive and in my home. Very bad publicity for me."

That she believed. "What about—" She was going to ask the nature of Rodrigo's business but was interrupted by the arrival of the police.

"*Señorita. Señores.* This is Rodrigo Santiago?" The police chief marched in and waved two of his men to Rodrigo.

Rafe handed him over, and they cuffed him immediately and took him out.

"Your guests will be coming with me as

well," the man said to Martinez. "They've been cleared." He turned to them at last. "You are free to leave. You'll need to sign some papers and collect your belongings."

"Gracias, señor," Isabelle said, and did not give voice to her frustration with being held this long for no good reason. Their stay at the Martinez estate had been productive, after all. And there was no sense in antagonizing the police now and giving them an excuse to drag things out.

"Thank you for your hospitality, Señor Martinez." She gave the man a polite smile.

"Muchas gracias, señor." Rafe nodded to the man before turning to follow the policeman outside.

"Good trick in that shed," she said as they walked down the stairs side by side. "Effective way to make Rodrigo talk. I never saw you take that bullet out of the gun."

He looked at her for a second before responding. "I didn't."

RAFE KEPT HIS EYE on the road, pushing the rental to its limits.

"Hey, didn't that sign say Cedra?" Isabelle

stifled a yawn and turned after the road post they'd flown by.

By the time they'd gotten everything squared away and their belongings back, it had been morning. She was probably missing her night of sleep but had been able to catch a few hours of shut-eye here and there while he drove.

"We should stop there," she said.

He thought about that for a few seconds.

Cedra, the town where he'd grown up, where his family lived, was only five miles ahead. Dusk was falling and he had to stop for gas anyhow. Except he hadn't planned on stopping in Cedra.

They'd wasted nearly four hours when they'd stopped for lunch and someone had stolen the back tires off their car. Finding replacements had been an adventure.

"I thought we could keep going until Malani and get a hotel room there."

"Wouldn't you want to see your family?" Her voice held faint traces of surprise.

"Some other time. We better hurry," he said, knowing how illogical that was. It made no difference whether they stopped for rest in Cedra or Malani, they would have to stop at some point.

What would Isabelle think of his mother, his siblings? She came from a well-to-do family; his family lived in a neighborhood that was one step above the slums. He had offered to move them on several occasions, but his mother was a traditional woman. She would not leave the house she'd grown up in. That was where the memories were, she'd said. That was where the happiness of the family came from.

And, oddly, he understood it. He could never come home to any other place like he went home there during his rare visits. To him, each carved beam, the cellar, the attic, the dusty backyard, all brought back myriad memories. But how would Isabelle see it all? And what would they think of her?

"You keep in touch a lot?" she asked.

"We talk on the phone. I visit at least once a year." And he sent money in between. He loved them, missed them, but he had another life someplace else, a life that didn't put them in danger, a life his mother was proud of. Still, fifteen years was a long time; they weren't as close as before. They knew little of his life in Miami, of the man he had become.

And it occurred to him, that when it came right down to it, nobody really knew the man he had become. He'd worn the carefree, foot-loose bachelor persona for so long—in part for cover, in part because having a life without outside complications was an advantage for his job—that even he barely recognized the man who was now reacting to Isabelle in unexpected ways.

We've been working together for three years and I hardly know you, Isabelle had said.

And that was true, too. He had many friends but no best friend, nobody who could claim he knew Rafe Montoya well. At the beginning, he'd kept his relationships superficial out of necessity. He wasn't proud of his past and hadn't cared to share it. Then as time went by, he had slipped into certain patterns, became, if not happy, then at least comfortable enough in them to let things stay as they were.

None of this had ever bothered him before. He hadn't given thought to it before Isabelle said she didn't know him at all. She made him look at things with a fresh eye. And he didn't like all that he saw.

He wanted Isabelle to know him.

Why?

She was important to him. It didn't have anything to do with any kind of "crisis," midlife or otherwise, he realized suddenly. She was a good person—honest, brave, the type he would want to hang out with more than just once in a while at a party. He wanted to have long talks with her. She was real, un-apologetic, tough.

She had intrigued him from the moment they'd met. He was attracted to her. Who wouldn't be? He was a healthy man and there was nothing wrong with his vision. And going on this trip together, spending 24/7 in each other's company, took his attraction to a new level.

Her constant presence had got under his skin until he could think of nothing else but her soft body under his. And beyond that, he had gotten to know her better, and with each little thing he liked her more.

She was the first person in a very long time whom he wanted to get closer to. He wanted to spend time with her once they were back in Miami, time outside of the office: hanging out, going places together, talking things over. She was a sharp one, a good person to bounce things off of.

He didn't want whatever they had between them to end up like all his brief affairs had. This time he wanted more, and he was willing to control his mad urges to rip her clothes off every time they were together to get it. He didn't want to give the impression that was all he cared about, especially since she already seemed plenty jaded about his past.

Night was falling and he turned on his headlights.

All he would have to do was keep his pants zipped for a few days longer, prove to her that this time it was different, she was different than anyone he'd ever had an interest in. He would court her properly. Win her heart.

He wanted her in his life. He wanted to share dinners, go to places together. He wanted her body, too, with a burning urgency, but he was prepared to ignore that for now until he convinced her that she was more to him than just another brief affair based on sex.

She was probably cautious for another reason as well. They worked together. If things didn't pan out, it wasn't as if they could go their separate ways and never see each other again. So it was a risk—but, by God, what they could have was worth taking a chance on.

HE WAS PLOTTING something, Isabelle thought, but let him take his time. He'd tell her sooner or later. He was probably trying to figure out the best way of approaching Maggie.

"So you don't mind hanging around me?" he asked out of the blue in a voice that was a little off.

Was this a trick question? "You have your moments," she said cautiously.

"How do you feel about kids?"

Her heart about stopped. Her brain insisted that she was hallucinating. She was staring at him, she knew, but she couldn't stop. "Kids?"

"If we stop to see my family, you'll probably have to share a bed with the girls." He seemed to have made up his mind about something and appeared more relaxed.

"Don't get into a tickling match with them. They are merciless."

"Okay," she said. The man was full of surprises.

He nodded, and after a few minutes put his turn signal on and pulled off the main highway toward Cedra.

In twenty minutes, he was stopping in front of a rambling home near the center of town, in a neighborhood she wouldn't have felt comfortable visiting alone.

The row of tightly built homes, some mud brick, some stone, seemed to be elbowing each other out of the way for space, reaching toward the sky with second and even third stories that looked like they'd been put in place with little forethought for stability or safety. The moon reflected off roofs that were either made of plastic tarps or some sort of plant fibers. The Montoya house seemed the best, with the whole roof actually standing, and the house built of real brick and good, straight lines that suggested the involvement of at least a half-competent architect.

"Prepare for the inquisition," Rafe said. "It's been a while since I brought home a girl."

"I'D BE HAPPY TO HELP." Isabelle followed Rosina, Rafe's sister, to the old-fashioned kitchen with its avocado-color fridge that kicked in from time to time and made enough noise for a small tractor. "We've been sitting in the car for hours. It feels good to be moving around."

Rosina, a true Latin beauty, flashed an unsure smile, perhaps worried about putting a guest to work.

Isabelle went straight to the sink and washed her hands. "What can I do?"

Realizing that her offer wasn't a token politeness, Señora Montoya gave her some strips of meat to roll in batter.

Both women's eyes kept returning to Rafe over and over again as they bustled about the kitchen.

"You miss him a lot," Isabelle observed.

Señora Montoya, a petite woman whose sharp brown eyes commanded respect, nodded. "I'm happy for him to be where he is. It is a good place for my son."

"Have you ever thought of maybe moving to Miami?" From the way Rafe was talking intently to his brother Eduardo in the living room while fending off nieces and nephews who were leaping at him from every direction, it was clear that he missed his family, too. Every once in a while, he caught a kid and messed him up, flipped him over backwards, tugged a ponytail on one of the girls, blew some raspberries on a toddler's belly.

He looked relaxed and happy, the hard edge that always seemed to be part of him almost completely gone. The other Rafe, the high-intensity, crime-fighting-machine took her breath away. This one melted her heart.

"Miami seems very far away," Rosina said. "Maybe when the bambinos are older we'll visit."

"Ladera is not a bad country," Señora Montoya added. "There might be a lot of bad things here, some bad people. But if all the good ones left, what would happen then?" She stirred something in a pot. "We stay and make it better."

"We help with the food pantry at the mission," Rosina explained. "Rafe sends things."

"Really?" Isabelle glanced at him, surprised. That was a side of him she'd never guessed.

Rosina nodded. "Books, too. He started a

community library. He says in Florida libraries sometimes sell off their old books by the paper bag, a dollar or two a bag. He goes around on Saturdays and gets as many as he can and ships them here—especially books in Spanish." She deftly drained a giant portion of oddly shaped noodles.

Saturdays. Isabelle winced. Rafe had a thing about not taking on Saturday assignments unless it was absolutely necessary. Just a month or so ago she had made some cutting remark to him about it, *God forbid one of their projects cut into his partying time,* or something along those lines.

"There aren't enough libraries?"

"Some, but they're afraid poor people might come in and steal books to sell them. To go in you have to pay a fee. Not many people have money for the membership, or to buy books. They come to our free library from very far away. Even teachers and doctors come to do research." Rosina's eyes brimmed with pride.

Isabelle always thought Rafe had stayed in Miami because it wasn't safe for him in Ladera, because he'd built a good life for himself there. But he was here now. He'd visited regularly, if not too often. Whatever troubles he'd had fifteen years ago, she was pretty sure the man he was now could handle any lingering enemies. Perhaps he stayed in Miami, away from the family he so obviously loved, because that was the best way for him to help the most.

Something inside her went soft. And when she realized she must be looking at him with that close-to-hero-worship admiration that glinted in Rosina's and Senora Montoya's eyes, she shook her head with a half smile and turned back to cooking.

RAFE PLAYED WITH the children and talked with Eduardo, but beneath it all was aware of every move Isabelle made in the kitchen. Having her in the house he'd grown up in went beyond strange. But it was also, somehow, incredibly right, like a lost piece of a mystic puzzle suddenly falling into place.

His family sensed it, too. Back in the day when he'd brought a girl home, his mother and sister would take turns giving her the evil eye. Yet, here was Isabelle, a foreigner, and

within ten minutes she was making empana-
das with them in the kitchen as if she'd
always done it.

Dinner was a lively affair, everybody
trying to catch up with him, telling him
stories, even repeating ones they'd already
told him over the phone. Sharing was different face-to-face, he supposed.

"Will you come fishing with us, *tío* Rafe?"

"It's too late for fishing," he said as their
father had always said. It was part of the ritual.

"*Tío,* it is Friday. No school tomorrow."

"It's too late, you'll fall asleep and fall in
the water."

The children protested and ran circles around
the table to prove just how awake they were.

"It's dark." Eduardo shook his head.

"*Padre,* dark is the best. We light a small
candle and the fish will come to see."

They kept up the bargaining for another
ten minutes before giving in. The children
rushed off for the poles and buckets in the
shed and ran ahead.

"Don't stay out late," Rosina called after
them as they walked off the veranda.

He glanced at Isabelle to see if she was

coming, but she shook her head. "I'll help clean up."

He stepped outside. *Diosmío,* it was good to be home. The short walk to the lake felt like a trip back in time, although there were more boats on it now, fancier. The rich, on the other side, were apparently getting steadily richer.

"All is well?" he asked.

Eduardo nodded. "And you? The work you do it's dangerous, *sí?*" He glanced toward the side of Rafe's jacket.

So he'd noticed the gun. Rafe wasn't surprised. Eduardo rarely missed anything. He hadn't wanted to bring the weapon into the house but didn't dare leave it in the car in case it was broken into during the night. He had emptied it, though, as a precaution, and tucked it out of sight in the small hallway while he'd been playing with the kids.

"Sometimes," he nodded.

"More dangerous than it should be for a security guard at weddings?" Eduardo was looking at him, clearly worried. "Your old—" he started to say then hesitated.

"My old ways are done with." Rafe cut

him off. "Some people are in trouble. We are helping them, that's all."

"Your partner, the woman, you trust her?" Eduardo asked after a moment of silence.

He wasn't taken aback by the question. Before he'd left Ladera, he had trusted the wrong people and it had nearly cost him his life, could have cost the innocent life of someone in his family.

The friends he had used to bring home back then, he had no business bringing into the house.

"I trust her as I trust you," he responded.

"I saw the way you were looking at her. If you trust her and love her, then why not marry her?" his brother asked suddenly and turned to face him.

Rafe was stunned by his brother's words. He hadn't got that far ahead yet, was still trying to figure out how to talk Isabelle into some kind of relationship with him at all.

"We work together," he said. It was the first thing that came to mind, too stunned to deny the "love" part.

The silence said *so?*

"How did you know you wanted to marry Juanita?"

Eduardo grinned, then grew serious. "Every time she wasn't with me it hurt. Here." He tapped the middle of his chest. "We are two of a kind. She was my best friend, you know. Still is. I hope we stay like that forever."

Marriage.

He shook off the thought. Marriage was for normal people with normal lives.

"My work is too dangerous."

"Seems to me like she's already in the danger with you."

His brother was right. Isabelle *was* already in danger with him. They *were* two of a kind.

Best friends, his brother had said about his wife, and Rafe realized all of a sudden that that's what he wanted when he'd thought about that elusive "something more" beyond his blinding physical need for her. He also wanted her to be his friend, to be his partner beyond work.

Diosmío, that did sound like marriage.

But would she have him? He wasn't even sure that at this stage he could talk her into a date. And maybe that was smart of her, considering his track record with dates.

"Isabelle is—" He shrugged, frustrated and growing unsure of it all. How could he explain? He knew without a doubt that she would make him happy. But could he do the same for her? What did he know about marriage? "She should have more. Better."

Eduardo raised an eyebrow and smiled again. "Never seen you worry about what a woman should have. You always knew what you wanted and went and got it."

He flashed his brother a look that had scared many a criminal into confession.

Eduardo grinned wider. "So you're in love with her?"

"*Padre! Padre!* I got a big one," one of the boys yelled, interrupting the friendly interrogation.

Then everything else was forgotten in the excitement as they both rushed to help, laughing and grabbing for the pole of the net as they'd done a hundred times before when they were both children, when their father was still alive, before their lives became a lot more complicated.

The first fish of the night was indeed a beauty, but the luck did not continue beyond it. Two hours later, they still had only that in the bucket, the children losing their enthusiasm and growing cranky, two of the boys picking a fight.

"To bed then. It's past time." Eduardo gave his fatherly verdict.

"But father, we'll have nothing to take to the market," they all protested.

Saturday was market day and the money the kids made from their Friday night catch they were allowed to keep and spend as they wished, a family tradition.

"I'll stay and see what I can do for you," Rafe said, surprising himself.

He wasn't ready to return to the family yet for more questioning. And there'd be that, he knew. Eduardo had been restrained. His mother and Rosina would be tougher to face. That's what he got for bringing Isabelle here after not crossing the threshold with a woman in fifteen years. She had come as a shock.

The noisy group trudged off, their voices growing fainter as they progressed down the street.

Something was different about this visit from all the others, but he couldn't put his finger on what it was. The place seemed imbued with nostalgia and melancholy; a flock of what-ifs swirled around him in the air.

What if he'd stayed? Would he be dead? Or would he have found a way out and be settled down now with a family, like Eduardo and Rosina?

Did he envy them?

Yes. A little.

Water splashed and drew his attention. One of the lines bobbed. He grabbed after the pole.

"Need help?" Isabelle's voice came from behind him and seemed to somehow bring balance to the night.

"Get the net." He wound the line, stopped, wound some more then waited for the fish to tire.

She was ready when the fish came close enough to the surface to be seen.

"What is it?" she asked, her tone of voice saying the rest—*ew, it's ugly.*

He laughed as he got the hook out of the fish's mouth and dropped it into the largest bucket, getting splashed. "A twenty-pound dorado. You should see it fried up in my mother's special spices. Much prettier that way, and tasty."

She stepped closer to the bucket and got a splash of water in the face for her trouble.

"Here." He stepped closer and used the sleeve of his shirt to dry her cheeks and brush the drops of water from her eyelashes.

The water lapped the shore, the sky clear above. Stars reflected in Isabelle's eyes, which looked black in the darkness. She smelled faintly like oranges, some natural cream she used on her face to protect it from the wind and sun of the Andes.

"It's beautiful here," she said.

His throat tightened for a second. To him, the poverty that lined this side of the small lake was home, comfortable even after fifteen years in Miami, the last few of which he'd spent in a nicely appointed condo. He hadn't expected anyone else who came from there to see past the shacks to the beauty that was in the people who lived here, the true beauty of the water, the sky and the sounds of the night.

"Beautiful," he repeated, looking at her, reaching back to her face again.

Then he caught himself just as his fingers would have curled around her cheek. *Friends.* He had to make sure that they became friends, not just lovers, so that they could build something beautiful, something lasting. That was the only way to keep her in his life. He gave her a pained grin, hoping she didn't realize how close he was teetering to the edge.

But she didn't seem to understand his inner fight with lust at all. Undermining his best intentions, she stepped forward and kissed him.

He was sinking fast.

Still, not one to give up anything without a fight, he raised his hands in an attempt of protest. She misunderstood the gesture and moved closer, her breasts pushing against his palms, bringing an end to his tenuous resistance.

A faint splash came from somewhere behind them. *Fish lines,* he remembered for a second, but then the thought slipped away.

He felt like the trees of the cloud forest, his feet on familiar ground, his head in a cloud called Isabelle Rush, a cloud that blinded and deafened him, swirled around until it swallowed all thought, leaving him only to feel. And the feelings she brought to the surface confused him, overwhelmed him, went against everything he had believed to be true about himself, his life, his future.

The first time, at the cave, he'd been blinded by passion, overtaken. This time, their lovemaking was an exploration—something magical, something unknown waiting for him that he had to discover.

He kissed a velvety soft spot below her ear. Had he noticed that before? Everything seemed new, the sharing of bodies gaining a whole other dimension.

She was small, petite. It had taken him over a year to realize she was a full head shorter than him, when one day she'd asked him to get a book off a tall shelf. Her personality, her inner strength wove an illusion around her that set her on equal footing with anyone.

And yet, just now, there was a fragility in her eyes that scared him. What if he ended up hurting her?

No. Not that. Never. No matter what he had to do. If he thought he might, he'd give her up first.

He wrapped her in his arms as they folded to the ground.

Isabelle.

He buried his face in her hair, in the hollow of her neck as he kissed her skin, moved down, opening a path for himself, unbuttoning her shirt as he went.

Her fingers were in his hair, restless, going to his shoulders and back, tugging at his clothes. Then her breasts were bare, her nipples puckered from the cool of the night air. He warmed them in his mouth.

His body was wound so tightly, he barely held on to control. He measured the distance to her belly button in kisses.

Time was lost to the haze of pleasure. Then there was no more clothing to separate them, and they lay skin to heated skin. When he took her, she lifted up, impatient, her thick moan filling his brain, blocking everything else out. She moved with him, then over him.

Pleasure rose like the lake in the season of rain; it washed away the walls he'd built around his heart, his soul.

"Isabelle."

Her name was all he could think, say, when they lay tangled and gasping for air. *Isabelle.*

Clouds drifted across the sky, in a steady line gliding toward the west.

She rose first, pulled away, reached for her clothes in a somewhat uncoordinated movement. She wouldn't look at him.

And he could see that something was wrong. She was probably regretting their lovemaking again, already classifying it as a mistake, moving away to someplace from where he might not be able to bring her back.

Diosmío, it looked bad, the way he kept grabbing her and taking her, as if that was all he wanted. Here in the open, on the grass trampled by his nephews, where anyone could have come and seen them. What had he been thinking?

He could not lose her. He was not going to let her put some professional distance back between them. He needed her in his life, though admitting that didn't come easily.

He wanted her, all of her. He wanted everything.

"I'm sorry. I'm sorry." He rushed to say

the words. "I didn't mean it like that. Please." He reached a hand toward her. "Let us be friends."

Chapter Eight

Let's just be friends.

God, the words hurt. He was done with her that quickly. If she'd had any hope that things would be different this time, with her, he sure set the record strait. *Be friends.*

"Yeah. Okay." She pressed the words through her burning throat.

She had opened her heart. She hadn't wanted to. She knew better. But damn if he didn't sucker her in. All the kindness, the old-fashioned charm, his strength, the glimpse he had allowed into his past, into his family— she'd thought she was getting to know him, that they were getting to know each other, that this was somehow, by some miracle, leading somewhere.

She swallowed and turned from him. She'd

been acting like an idiot for long enough. She wasn't going to top it off by crying.

Bad enough that she'd gone and fallen in love.

Isabelle closed her eyes and swallowed the pained groan that was bubbling up in her throat.

Fallen in love.

When? Had to be before the cave. She wouldn't have slept with him in the first place if she hadn't had any feelings for him.

This mission was to blame. They were spending too much time together. The attraction she'd been ignoring and denying for years had had a chance to grow into something more despite her better judgment.

She had fallen in love with Rafe Montoya.

She hadn't realized until just a few minutes ago, until he had called out her name so thick with emotion that it made her heart lurch in response. The heart that would soon be broken because along the way she had at one point given it to him. And he had no idea what else to do with hearts. She'd seen him enough with other women to know that.

God, she was an idiot.

It was fun, now let it go. Even while she

thought that, she knew she couldn't do it. Her family was full of one-man women. They fell once and they fell hard. It was her own rotten luck that she had to fall for Rafe, who was already dumping her before she even had her underwear back on.

"I'm going back to the house," she said, keeping her voice even, yanking on her clothes. "We have to get up early in the morning."

She bit her lip to counteract the tingling aftereffects of their lovemaking. Sex, she corrected herself. That's all it had been to him. Lord, but at the time it had felt like more. It had felt like everything, a melting of minds and hearts.

Showed what she knew.

She had, afterward, been a little embarrassed about throwing herself at him like that, was going to make some silly joke of it just before he doused her with the cold water of his words.

Friends.

She stepped into her shoes and stood, then left him without looking back, as if what had happened between them meant as little to her as it had meant to him. She didn't want him to see the truth in her eyes. Loving him was her problem. She would deal with it.

RAFE STEPPED ON THE GAS, focusing on traffic, but his thoughts were on Isabelle, who sat silently next to him, watching the houses they passed, the tourists, the street vendors and the beggars.

He'd messed up. He felt the shift in her.

Damn it.

What the hell was wrong with him? Why had he got so bad at this all of a sudden?

Because Isabelle Rush was different. And, surprisingly, *he* was different when he was with her. What happened between them, whether she'd still be in his life in a couple of years, mattered. He didn't know what to do with that. Had no practice in it. Zero.

"You have a nice family," she said without looking at him, making polite small talk.

This is what they'd come to.

"Yeah," he said. If she brought up the weather he was going to bang his head against the steering wheel.

He wanted to reach for her hand but didn't think it was a good idea. Every time they as much as brushed together, his body demanded instant replay of the previous night.

Man, he'd screwed that up.

She'd slept on the pullout couch in the living room with his nieces, while he had spent the night in the hammock on the veranda. He'd barely got any rest, missing the soft sound of her breathing, her scent.

And he'd better get used to missing it. On this mission, they pretty much spent twenty-four hours a day together. All that would end once they were back in Miami.

"When are we supposed to check in with Rachel next?" he asked.

"No set time. After we talk to Maggie." Isabelle turned away from the window and looked at the map on her lap. "Looks like we're almost there. You need to take the next right."

He'd been to Malani a few times a very long time ago, but the place had changed a lot—new streets had been added, new buildings had replaced old ones. He drove while Isabelle read the map and directed him, and they hadn't made a single wrong turn. They made a good team.

"There," she said.

The building sat above the street, five stories high and a whole block wide. A pretty walkway separated it from the road, edged with flowering bushes.

"Massive." She was out of the car as soon as he shut the engine off.

Thick black bars protected the small windows, the yellow masonry of the walls peeling here and there, revealing the stone beneath.

Hospital De Los Problemas Inocentes, proclaimed a mosaic sign above the entry. *Hospital For The Problems of the Innocent,* a very nice way they said mental institution in Ladera.

They'd both seen the place before on the video recording Ethan Whitehawk, another agent who worked for Miami Confidential, had made during an earlier visit. He had got in by pretending to be a doctor from the Global Research Center. His interview with Maggie had turned up little else than that she knew Dr. Ramon, the man who had attempted to kill Sonya's limo driver and then had committed suicide when apprehended by Rafe and Julia—another Miami Confidential agent. Rafe still felt responsible for that. He hadn't expected Ramon to make a move that drastic.

Maggie had known Dr. Ramon. She'd been in his care before he'd left for Miami. Isabelle seemed convinced Maggie knew a hell of a lot more than she let on.

"Hard to believe someone from here could pull off a kidnapping in Miami," he said. "When I think about the number of people involved, the coordination. A place like this—" He shrugged, then shook his head. "I'm betting she's watched pretty closely. I don't think she could have done it."

"That's because you tend to underestimate women," she said sweetly.

He looked at her, held her gaze. "I never underestimated you."

He'd known from day one that she could get to him without half trying. And now she had.

There was a flicker of emotion in her eyes that passed too swiftly to be identified. Then she turned from him and started down the sidewalk. He watched her legs, the way her hips swayed as she walked—all feminine but not coyly so.

"Hope Rachel is right and we're not going

to have any trouble getting in," he said when he caught up with her.

"We are lucky she was with Juan when I called and he offered to call ahead," she said.

And she *was* right. Ethan had had to go to the trouble of making up a fake background and a fake ID.

But because Juan was the one who'd committed Maggie and he still paid her bills, apparently, as far as the place was concerned he was still her guardian, despite the divorce. And if he said that friends of his were going to stop by to check on her for him, that was okay with the institute.

He pushed the heavy front door open, and saw a scene familiar from Ethan's video: uniformed staff going about their business, an upscale hospital that obviously catered to the rich of the country.

"Buenos días." A guard sat by a small, square desk just inside the door.

They showed their passports for ID, signed the visitors' log, and, as they had no packages that would have required a search, they were passed through.

Despite the pastel-colored walls, the

corridor that led to the middle of the building had an uncomfortable feel to it that made him uneasy. Odd how different it was to experience the place in person than on the computer screen.

A patient meandered by, wearing an expensive robe over his silk pajamas, his eyes vacant as he turned down another hallway, probably on his way for some kind of scheduled treatment.

"I don't like this place." Isabelle rolled her shoulders. "Can't imagine having a family member here and not doing everything to get her out. If Maggie's father is as rich and powerful as he seems to be, why not have her treated at home? They could certainly afford private care."

She was definitely on to something. He looked at the bars on the windows.

The place didn't look like a prison but sure as hell was the same in its essence—complete loss of freedom. He felt sorry for Maggie. No matter how plush the place seemed compared to other institutes of this type, being confined here year after year with nothing but bad memories had to be a living hell.

"What?" Isabelle caught his mood.

He shrugged. "I don't enjoy putting the screws to some unfortunate woman."

"Good. I can be the bad cop then?" She seemed ready to tackle their mission with full steam.

"Be my guest."

A door opened ahead, and a middle-aged woman stepped out wearing a dark-blue uniform. Her dark hair was clipped short, her eyes remaining somber despite the polite smile that stretched her thin lips.

"*Bienvenidos Señor y Señorita. Soy Rita Marquez.* I'm the director on Señora DeLeon's floor. I've been expecting you." She gave them a tight smile as she walked forward, dragging her right foot a little. "Please, follow me." She slipped a key from her pocket, opened a padded door and stepped through to another hallway.

Rooms opened on both sides, about a dozen of them, a small common area at the end with armchairs and tables. Everything was clean and tastefully decorated, art reproductions lining the walls, although Rafe noticed that the frames had no glass in them.

"Does Señora DeLeon have many visitors?

Her family still comes every weekend?" Rafe asked, remembering that Maggie had told Ethan about some family visits.

"*Sí, Señor.* Her niece comes every Sunday. The young girl is planning on taking up the veil and becoming a nun of Saint Margaret. I think Señora DeLeon has become her mission," she said with an expression of approval. She knocked on one of the doors but opened it without waiting for response.

He glanced at the doorknob—the only keyhole was on the outside.

Maggie sat in a chair by the window. There were dark shadows under her eyes that couldn't be covered up by any expensive makeup, shadows that hadn't been there a few weeks ago on Ethan's video. She barely glanced at the people entering her room, turning her attention to the outside world again.

"*Buenos días, Señora DeLeon,*" Isabelle greeted her, her voice firmly professional. "Hope you are feeling well. I'm Isabelle Rush. My friend Rafe Montoya and I are here on Juan's behalf."

"Juan has remembered me at last?" She looked at them again, and this time her attention stayed.

Her long black hair was pulled up into a sleek twist, her nails done in pale pink. He caught the scent of expensive perfume. Maggie DeLeon lived well in captivity.

Juan was paying for her care but wasn't sending her extra money beyond that. The only other option was that her family was keeping her in money.

"Should I stay?" the director asked no one in particular.

Maggie looked at Rafe and cocked a black eyebrow, and for a moment he could see something in her eyes, something sharp and calculating.

"That won't be necessary," he said.

When the door closed and they were alone, he pulled out a chair for Isabelle then took one for himself across from Maggie DeLeon.

"Señora DeLeon—"

"So you work for Juan? You've come a long way to see me." She pulled a pack of cigarettes from her pocket and lit one.

Isabelle made a face at the smoke but didn't

say anything. Good, they wanted the woman to talk and didn't want to antagonize her.

"You keep up with news on your ex, *señora?*" she asked.

"He's on TV from time to time." Maggie shrugged.

"Then you know that his fiancée was kidnapped?"

"Seems like somebody interrogated me about that a while ago." Maggie looked disinterested. "I have nothing new to say."

"We do. Your cousin was killed at a shootout connected to the kidnapping. Perhaps you heard that from your niece already?" Isabelle asked.

A muscle jumped in Maggie's cheek. She said nothing.

Isabelle pushed on. "Funny how people around you tend to end up badly. Dr. Ramon killed himself rather than face charges of the attempted murder of Ms. Botero's driver. Quite a coincidence isn't it? All these people you know connected to the kidnapping."

Maggie's face went a shade whiter. Her gaze cut to Rafe for a second, full of emotion, then away again. The effort it took to keep her voice from shaking was visible in the bunched muscles of her neck, in her white-knuckled hand that gripped the arm of the chair.

"It would be unfortunate if anything happened to Sonya Botero." Isabelle wasn't about to let up on her. "If she's found safe and sound, it's one thing. If the rescue is too late… The U.S. will extradite all persons involved."

Maggie drew from her cigarette, refusing to look at Isabelle, keeping her gaze on Rafe. Did she expect him to step in and help? She was a strikingly beautiful woman; no doubt she had little trouble beguiling men in the past, Dr. Ramon perhaps being one of them if Isabelle was right, although Rafe could imagine things happening the other way around just as easily. Maggie was a patient in Ramon's care, at his mercy.

"We can help you if you help us," he said. "You need to help us find Sonya right now, before it's too late."

"American jails are not like Laderan hospitals. They don't work on the bribery system. You're not going to get any favors from the guards. If you want smokes, you'll have to play nice with some very nasty inmates." Isabelle kept the tight smile on her face. "Conspiracy to kidnapping and murder, accessory to murder." She went on and kept listing the possible charges.

"You can't pin that on me," Maggie said, still holding her voice even.

"We already have. You have a very special niece, a little on the naïve side, though. She didn't realize just how much trouble she can get into on your account for passing on those messages. Well, she does now and she doesn't want to go down in your place." Isabelle bluffed like the best of them.

Maggie set her cigarette down. She seemed to be wavering.

"Murder is a nasty thing," Isabelle pushed. "Our police take it very seriously. You'll be tried in Miami, where Sonya is something of a celebrity. It will be a very public trial." She stood and stepped closer to the woman. "You think you'll be able to bribe an American judge?"

"Shut up." Maggie's voice rose, then she sank back into the chair and rubbed her forehead, showing signs of stress now. Again, she looked to Rafe for help.

He kept his face hard and his arms folded. This was Isabelle's show, and she was doing a damned fine job of it.

"Where is she?" Isabelle rounded on Maggie, her body language screaming she meant business.

"I don't know."

Was there a hint of desperation in her voice?

"Things would go much better for you if you did. Look, we already know you are involved. At this stage, there's only one question: will we find Sonya dead or alive?" Isabelle paused for effect. "Alive would work much better for everyone involved."

Maggie shook her head and started smoking again.

"We know your family kept her near the army base. Where have they moved her?"

Maggie was turning whiter yet. "I don't know."

"I have a hard time believing that. I'm sure the judge will feel the same."

And then all of a sudden color flooded Maggie's face, and without warning she hurled the ashtray at Isabelle's head, missing it by an inch.

Rafe moved in to restrain her as she lunged forward.

She struggled against him, screaming. "I don't know where the hell the bitch is, all right? Do you think I care what happens to me? Do you think a day goes by since you bastards drove Ramon to his death that I don't wish I were dead with him?"

Then the heat of her outburst was done and she collapsed against his chest, crying now. He eased her back into her chair but stayed by her side.

"Who was watching Sonya in that hut by the base? Where is she now?"

Maggie straightened her back and wiped her eyes. "I can't help you. I'm glad I don't know where they took her. If I don't know, there's nothing you can do to get it out of me. Then she will die."

"They?" Isabelle came closer. "Who are they?"

"Some men my cousin worked with. I don't know them. Never did. When he... When he was murdered by your people, his friends decided they wanted the ransom for themselves." She was looking straight at them now, her gaze boiling with hate. "I hope they don't get a cent of the money. I hope they hurt that *bruja* before they kill her. I hope Juan will suffer."

She shot out of her chair, and Rafe stood ready to handle her if she turned violent again, but all she did was stride to the window. "My baby died, you know. I was sick, and my baby died. And Juan punished me for it. He locked me up. I wanted to die. I wanted to get out of here, I wanted to get him back. He would never even visit."

She paced, moving as though in a trance. "The good side of my family, the one he liked, the one that gave money for his elections, they offered to get me out of here. Then I thought, no. I would stay in the misery he put me in, and I would show him the hell that lived inside me, I would let it swallow him. Nobody would suspect me in here, nobody would think of me when he was destroyed. So the bad part of my family, the ones he was ashamed of, the branch he was afraid to acknowledge in public, we made a plan."

"Why now?" Isabelle asked. "Why wait this long?"

Rafe could see the hate and lunacy swirling in her gaze as she said, "I wanted him to have something that was worth taking." Then she turned and walked back toward the window, but as she passed by Rafe she grabbed him by the arm. "I want him destroyed the way he destroyed me." Her words were gaining passion.

"He didn't destroy you," Rafe said, feeling only pity for the woman.

"Is he suffering? Is he going crazy yet?" she demanded.

He peeled her fingers from him and gently pushed her back into the chair. "We've got what we came for," he said to Isabelle, and she nodded.

"You think they'll extradite her?" he asked, once they were walking down the hall toward the front entrance, hurrying, impatient to contact Rachel with the new information, wanting to get out of the building and its oppressive atmosphere.

"It's not worth the effort. She is insane. No jury would convict her. It's sad, you know." Her face softened as she spoke.

When he put an arm around her shoulders in a friendly gesture, she didn't pull away.

Then they were out in the light, in the open, but the mood of the building still clung to them.

Isabelle dug out her phone and was dialing already. "Hi, it's me. Any news?" She listened for a second. "We hit a dead end here. Sonya is with friends of Maggie's cousin, Jose Fuentes." And since Fuentes was dead and couldn't be questioned, that information was not much to go by. "Can you ask Juan again if he might have remembered anything else about Fuentes? The few times they met, did he see the man hang out with anyone whose name he recalls?" She listened for a few moments. "Okay. We'll stay safe, don't worry. You do the same."

"Rachel will check into it," she said as she hung up.

"Anything new?"

"Not much. Sonya's father is doing pretty badly. Juan is going nuts that Sonya is still missing." She dug through her back pocket and tossed a handful of pesos into the tin plate of a street beggar who was setting up on the sidewalk.

They got back into the car, and he put the key in the ignition but didn't turn it.

"You were right about Maggie," he said.

She looked at him, shrugged. "Wasn't much help, was it? She couldn't give us anything."

Frustration tightened her mouth. She wanted this to work, she wanted it badly. He loved that about her—how much she cared.

"Anyway—" he said, and turned the key "—just wanted to say that for the record."

A ghost of a smile tugged her lips into a more relaxed line. "Appreciate it." She leaned back in her seat, closing her eyes for a moment, then turned back to him and gave voice to her frustration at last. "I know we are close. What are the chances Juan comes through with something new?"

"Slim to none. Sean Majors questioned him pretty exhaustively when Fuentes was killed." And as much as he hated that he had to share his investigation with Botero's top security guy, he had to admit Sean was all right. He doubted the man would miss much.

Rachel had checked all arrest records at the time as well, but Fuentes had had only one brush with the law before and he'd been apprehended alone. No matter how hard Miami Confidential agents looked, their search didn't net any other names in connection with the man.

He put the car in gear, and Isabelle snapped on her seat belt. "Any other ideas how to find these friends of Fuentes?"

He had plenty of ideas but none of them terribly healthy. To get some dirt on Fuentes, they would have to enter the Laderan underworld, poke around in a territory that belonged to drug lords and crime bosses, some of whom probably still held pretty serious grudges against him.

"I might have some connections," he said slowly, hating to take Isabelle into that kind of danger but seeing no way around it.

The next step had to be taken with care. It could lead them to Sonya. But it could just as easily get them killed.

Chapter Nine

Isabelle checked her gun twice, made sure the holster Rafe had gotten for her earlier that morning was set to a perfect fit. He stood at the end of his own bed, doing the same.

They had gone fifty miles back north after they'd left Maggie and stopped just one town short of Cedra. He needed to be back around his old connections, but didn't want to bring any harm to his family, so they stayed the night at the Hotel Iguana.

They had shared a room for the sake of safety, but had separate beds. *Friends.*

She hated how much the rejection hurt. Her fault entirely, with no one else to blame. She had known from the get-go how he was with women. She had known it, but on this trip, somehow, as she had got to know him better, some unreasonable hope had taken over, that maybe she'd been wrong. She could have sworn she'd got glimpses of a different man, that passion like what they had between them could not exist without equally strong emotions behind it. She'd been wrong, of course. Most likely, the only emotion he was experiencing was the urgent desire to back out of whatever they had started.

She was a grown woman. She would handle her disappointment. She had more important things to worry about than her bruised heart—like saving Sonya Botero's life.

"You should—" Rafe started to say, and from the cautious look in his eyes she knew exactly where he was going.

"I'm not staying."

"These are rough people." His shoulders seemed stiff with tension, no trace of his easygoing manner now.

"Yeah, I know. I put in my time at the DEA just like you, remember? I can handle it."

"That's not the point." He sank back onto the bed, looking tired all of a sudden as he rubbed a hand over his face before lifting his gaze to hers again. "Look, the people I used to hang with, we didn't leave each other on the best terms. It's not the kind of business you can simply quit and walk away from. I made enemies."

"I got that already," she said. "That's why I'll be providing backup."

She half expected him to use some stupid excuse—such as she'd be a distraction—and was prepared to be offended and rip in to him if that's all he thought of her. Instead, he said, "And if something happens to the both of us? Who will get Sonya?"

That gave her pause.

Even if Rachel could send in a new team immediately, they'd likely be too late. The mission was down to the wire. They either got to Sonya within the next twenty-four hours or they'd be giving their condolences to Juan.

They had one chance, this chance, and had to risk everything on it.

"Your connections are our only viable lead," she said, feeling more somber by the minute. "If something happens to you, if they don't help, there's nothing I can do to get Sonya anyway."

"But at least you'd be safe." He watched her

with that rare intensity of his that always took her breath away, his irises darkening to black, the air between them crackling with tension.

She pulled away from that mesmerizing hold with tremendous effort. "Staying safe is not my main objective. I don't see *you* playing anything safe. What if one of these old buddies of yours decides to shoot you on sight?"

"I hope I can reason with them."

"Well, I don't know them. They have nothing against me. Maybe I can charm them with my sunny personality. Who's to say that won't work better?"

"It might." The fight seemed to go out of him all of a sudden, and he gave her a rueful grin, took a deep breath. "In any case, it's your decision. I'm just saying, I'd rather see you safe."

"Your preference is noted." She pulled on a light jacket that covered her gun. "But I'm still going."

"Yeah." He shook his head. "I pretty much figured."

He headed for the door, unlocked it and opened it for her.

"So, what are you going to tell them?"

she asked as she passed him and stepped out into the narrow hallway, between the lavender-colored walls that displayed ceramic iguanas hanging off carpentry nails every couple of feet.

"Not that I'm in law enforcement, that's for sure." He pulled the door closed, made sure it was locked.

"Private security?"

He nodded. "I'd rather keep things as murky as I can. Don't want to mention Sonya's name at all. If I absolutely have to divulge details, I'll say Juan had dealings with a company I provide security for. After the kidnapping he asked for my help since he knew I was originally from Ladera."

They reached the lobby, empty save the clerk, who had his nose buried in the computer, passed the single couch provided for the benefit of guests should there ever be a line at check-in, which she seriously doubted. The round table in the middle displayed the mother of all ceramic iguanas with psychotic green eyes, like the bottoms from a pair of beer bottles.

"So, where are we going first?" she asked as she shook her head at the local "art."

"To an old friend of mine, if he's still alive. I thought we could drive around his usual hangouts, see if he's still there, or if not maybe I'll spot someone else I used to know," he said, and held the door of the SUV open for her.

"Sounds like a plan. And who is this guy?"

"Enrique Gonzales." He pulled out of the parking lot after the donkey cart got out of their way.

She leaned back in her seat and watched the street vendors on the sidewalks, an old beggar on the corner, a gang of teenagers, old women with loaded baskets—probably coming from a nearby market.

"Do you miss it?" she asked.

"Sometimes." He turned down a street that led to a narrow square with the statue of the cross in the middle.

People had heaped flowers at the foot of the cross, some of the blooms looking several weeks old, others as fresh as if they'd come that morning. Candle stubs and frozen drippings of wax framed the base.

The houses behind the small square were different from the semi-affluent neighborhood their hotel belonged to. They passed nothing but duplexes, row homes and apartment rentals.

This house is not for sale, someone had painted across the front of one of the nicer-looking homes. She'd seen signs like that at a few other places before. "How odd is that?" she asked now. "Does that mean that all the other houses *are* for sale?"

"Scams," he said. "There are a lot of them going around. People are afraid someone might advertise and sell their house without their knowledge. The signs warn prospective buyers."

"That's crazy." She scanned the rest of the houses for more signs now, but the neighborhood was getting more and more dilapidated the farther they went, and it seemed few worried here about anyone wanting their place. "Can you imagine someone knocking on your door telling you to move out because they own your home? What can people do when that happens?"

"Not much. The scams are operated by gangs. They have the police on their payroll."

He stepped on the brake to avoid a group of very dirty children running across in front of them. Seedy bars dotted the streetscape, the roads getting worse, the sidewalks more crowded. People sat on front porches in groups and looked at the slowly moving car with suspicion.

"Keep your gun handy, but don't let it show." Rafe scanned the street on both sides.

She sat up straighter and kept her mind on the dangers.

They made their way down to the next cross street, a larger thoroughfare, and used it to get to the next parallel street that looked very much like the first. They repeated the process a few times until they covered an area of about ten blocks.

"Nothing here," he said, and made his way back to the main road.

"On to the next hopeful location?"

He nodded. "There's a chop shop not too far."

Charming, she thought, and kept her eyes on the street, hoping they'd be able to avoid serious trouble before getting there.

The neighborhood he drove to turned out to be one very similar to the first they had searched, except this one contained some derelict businesses and factory yards, more industrial in nature. One of the larger abandoned parking lots had been converted into a city of shacks.

Four hoodlums lounged on a pile of bricks that might have been the guardhouse once, while a small child sat on the edge of the gutter nearby, dirty and unattended. A few shacks over, a man urinated against the chain-link fence. Repulsive, scary, heartbreaking—she had a hard time classifying her impressions as the smell of poverty and despair came through the cracked open window to fill the car.

She half hoped that Enrique wouldn't be here either, and they wouldn't have to get out. Maybe he took his business to a more civilized neighborhood these days.

But even as hope formed in her mind, Rafe stuck his head out and yelled, "Paco Loco!"

One of the hoodlums picked up his head, took one glance at the car and took off running in the opposite direction, dashing among the shacks.

Rafe slammed on the brake. "If you leave the car, it won't be here when we come back.

I don't want to be stuck here without it," he said as he put the car in Park and was already out the door before she could respond.

Fine. She shut the door behind him, remaining in her seat, and watched him tear after Paco. She locked the car and rolled the windows higher, leaving only a small gap open. By the time she turned her attention back to Rafe, he was out of sight. Paco's friends were watching her with interest.

She ignored them and tried her best not to look intimidated.

All will be well just as long as they stay where they are, she thought and watched one of them slide off the bricks, then another, then the last.

Not good.

They looked to be in their mid-twenties, a few scars here and there proving they'd seen the rougher side of life. They were guffawing, apparently egging each other on as they sauntered toward her.

Great. Perfect.

She slid over into the driver's seat and kept the car running.

"*¿Qué pasa, mamacita?*" The first guy

who reached her leaned his hip against the hood of the car.

"Waiting for a friend," she responded in Spanish.

"And who is your friend?" The tallest of the three bent to her window, his dark hair tied back with a dirty bandana.

"A friend of Paco."

"Paco didn't look it," he said while the third guy was trying her door.

"Stuck? Any friend of Paco is a friend of ours. Why don't you come out and play?" The words were said with an open leer.

Cold sweat ran down her back, but she kept her face composed, her expression unimpressed. She let her jacket fall back, let them see the gun.

"Oooh, we got here a tough *mamacita*. Heavy metal." The tall guy's smile widened as he pulled up his shirt and showed off a semiautomatic that made the Beretta Rafe had traded his watch for the night before look like a toy.

"You're not from around here. You a cop or something?" He measured her up.

"No."

"Then why is your friend chasing Paco?"

"Maybe he wants to give the boy a present."

"Oooh—" The one in the front separated himself from the hood. "*Mamacita* called Paco a boy."

They laughed, apparently enjoying the situation, the control they thought they had over her. They played with her like a couple of alley cats with an out-of-its-element mouse.

Where in the hell was Rafe? She really, really didn't want to have to shoot anybody.

Sadly, the chances of that doubled as the youngest looking of the three pulled his gun and pointed it at the car door. "Let's see if my key fits this lock," he said.

She went for her Beretta, but a sharp whistle interrupted the three bozos outside. Paco and Rafe were coming back, Paco's arm draped around Rafe's shoulder in a friendly gesture. Rafe's face was all smiley and the very picture of cordial conversation, but his eyes were on the men by the car, his free hand dangling over his gun.

"It's okay. An old friend," Paco called out in Spanish.

The hoodlums headed over to check out

Rafe. She let her gun slip back into the holster and relaxed against her seat, unlocked the doors. She wasn't sure what game Rafe was playing. He might need to get into the car in a hurry. She watched closely, ready to help him in any way, but he didn't seem to need her assistance.

The men chatted amicably for a while before the encounter ended with the three of them back on the brick pile, and Paco in the back of the SUV.

He was skinny, his face weather-beaten, about the same age as his buddies.

"You recognized him from fifteen years ago?" she asked in English once Rafe pulled away.

"He looks just like his father," he said.

Paco was talking on his cell phone rapidly. "Enrique is at the gas station behind the mission church," he said.

Rafe nodded and turned left at the next intersection. "You told him I was coming?"

The guy grinned. "I want to see if he recognizes you quicker than I did. You know, on first glance, I could've sworn you were cops."

They swapped stories along the way, most of

them sad ones—a list of people who'd died in street fights and from drugs, or were in prison.

She looked at Rafe and considered what a small miracle it was that he had become the man he was today. He'd had the wisdom to know back then where the road he was born on led, and he had the strength to leave it, to make his own destiny.

Millions and millions were born every day into circumstances such as his, but he had escaped, he had made a life for himself. He had saved his family; his continued support was making a huge difference in the lives of his nephews and nieces. None of them would have to sell their souls to the drug lords just so they could eat. And with both the DEA and Miami Confidential, he'd been on a number of extremely dangerous missions, gone undercover in the Bolivian cartels, risking his life to make sure someday the problem was stopped at the source.

Truth be told, she admired a great deal about the man.

Which wasn't exactly helpful in her quest of falling out of love with him.

"SO WHAT DO YOU WANT with Fuentes's men? Distributing his will, eh?" Enrique sat in the small backroom across a wobbly card table from Rafe, his eyes squinting from the smoke in the air. "I'm cautious, you understand," he said and kept one hand on his lap.

Rafe wondered if he still had that old revolver or if he'd finally given into progress and was holding a newer gun on him under the table. He wasn't overly concerned about the weapon. Between him and Isabelle, who stood a few feet behind him, they had Enrique covered.

"Cautious is smart. You wouldn't still be alive if you weren't."

Enrique nodded and poured another round of tequila with his left hand, spilling only a single drop. So his hands weren't as steady anymore, Rafe noted. The man might have managed to stay alive, but he had aged at least thirty years in the past fifteen. His hair had thinned and gone completely gray, although he still kept it pulled back in a ponytail. He had a couple of new scars on his face and

looked like his nose had been broken again
at least once since Rafe had last seen him.

Rafe emptied the shot glass, although the
alcohol was burning a hole in his stomach.
Still, to refuse would have been rude, and
very unlike the Rafe who Enrique had known
fifteen years ago. To demonstrate how much
he had changed would not have advanced his
cause. He needed to convince Enrique that he
was still the same, that he could be trusted,
that whatever Enrique told him wasn't going
to net him a drive-by or a firebomb flying
through his window.

"Fuentes had something that belongs to
my employer. I think his friends might have
it now. I'm here to get it back," Rafe said.

Revenge and working for an unforgiving
employer were things that people like
Enrique understood.

"Is there any money in this?" The man's
red-rimmed eyes narrowed.

They measured each other up, Rafe thinking
how much would be enough, Enrique probably
considering how much an employer who could
afford Rafe's services would be willing to pay.

"Yes," Isabelle said, speaking for the first

time since the introductions but right on cue, offering Enrique some hope and motivation.

"Depends on how good the information is," Rafe corrected as if she'd spoken too soon.

Enrique poured again but hesitated before picking up his glass. "Pedro Carrera, you remember him?"

"I do," Rafe said. How could he not? At one time, Pedro and he had been like brothers. "What is he doing these days?"

Enrique shrugged. "Growing up, branching out."

"With Fuentes?"

"Last I heard his new partner got popped somewhere in the States. Figured it was a botched delivery. His name was Fuentes if I remember it right."

Rafe leaned forward. They had their man, although he wished it was anyone else but Pedro Carrera. "You know where I can find Pedro?"

"I don't know where he hangs these days, but I might be able to find out where he'll be tonight. Friend of mine has a meeting with him."

"The information would be more than appreciated," Rafe said casually, not letting any indication of how desperately he wanted Pedro slip into his voice.

"He won't be happy if he finds out I sent you there. Same for my friend. They have business to take care of."

"I am not after anyone's business. I'm here to pick up a package and return it home."

"Maybe my friend's business is the package," he said, fishing for more information.

"You got friends in the human trade these days?" He lifted an eyebrow and let the disgust he felt show on his face.

Enrique spat on the floor. "No. Nasty business, that. Had an aunt kidnapped when I was a kid. They never brought her back."

Rafe nodded, knowing the story well and playing on it.

"Still, if Carrera finds out I sent someone to him..." Enrique tapped a finger on the table. "You don't know him. He came to be a big man since you disappeared."

"He won't know how I found him."

"Paco knows you came to me."

"I didn't tell him why I needed you. Just looking up an old friend."

This time when Enrique lifted his glass to his lips, he merely nibbled his drink. "I'll have to call around, make sure my information is correct. I'll have to ask favors."

Time to bring the negotiation home, the man was as softened up as Rafe could hope to get him. "How much?"

Enrique set his glass down and scratched the side of his nose with a dirty fingernail. "Ten thousand Laderan pesos."

Rafe nodded after a moment, although the amount seemed like extortion. He could have knocked it down to half, he figured, but didn't want to waste time with more bargaining.

"When will you have a location on him for sure?"

"In a couple of hours."

"You let me know as soon as you have it." He pulled a restaurant receipt from his pocket and wrote his cell phone number on it. "If your tip is any good, I'll pay you the full amount."

The man shook his head and watched him with the sly expression of a fox. He was probably wondering if he could have got more money out of the deal, thinking Rafe had agreed too easily. "You pay me the ten thousand now and get on the road to Maratiña. I'll give you the exact location on the phone as soon as I have it. It won't be long. You wait around, you might miss the meeting."

Maratiña.

Rafe hesitated only a moment or two before he got his billfold out and counted ten thousand Laderan pesos onto the table. He had got twenty out of the bank that morning, knowing he would be seeing Enrique, knowing how the old man worked.

Enrique slipped the money into a small drawer attached to the underside of the table. "Good luck to you, then," he said, then added, "Don't come back if Carrera is after you."

"Thank you for your help," Isabelle said, all ladylike and polite but turned back from the door. "Don't worry about Carrera. When we are done with him, he won't be bothering anyone." This time, she let the steel show in her voice.

Enrique's eyes widened in surprise.

Rafe bit back a smile. God, she was beautiful.

It was a good feeling, being with her, even if they were facing less than ideal circumstances at the moment. Once Sonya was safe, he would work on the rest, figure out a way to make it permanent. But first, they had to survive the next twenty-four hours.

Paco waited for them by the car outside. "Everything okay?"

"*Sí.* I was going to take you for a drink, seeing how you're all grown up, but something came up. I got a call I have to follow up on." Rafe patted his cell phone in his pocket then pulled out a hundred pesos and handed it to him. "You have a drink with your compadres for my health, *sí?*"

"Good health for a long time and lots of bambinos." Paco grinned at the bill then looked up at him with a wink.

"You need a ride back?"

"I'm good here. I thought of something I should check out while I'm up this way. *Adiós, amigo.*"

Rafe nodded, pretty sure that "something" involved the infamous street of prostitutes just a block away, Paco having that money in his pocket now. "Have fun. Stay safe," he called after him as Paco crossed the street.

"You must know Enrique pretty good to

just leave the money and walk away," Isabelle said, once they were back in their car.

"I could do that because he knows *me* pretty good," he said. If Enrique didn't deliver on his promise, he knew Rafe would be back.

"You know—" she said with a pensive look. "It's odd to think about the man you were and the man you are. The difference must be enormous. Did you hang out by the shacks in your younger days? I mean like Paco?"

"I've hung out at worse places than that," he said.

"It had to be hard to get out."

"Yeah," he said, and wondered if anyone ever could understand just how hard. He put the SUV in Drive and rolled down the street in the direction of their hotel. Time to pack up and move on.

"I mean," she continued, "I look at these people and think why not just get up and go someplace else, start new? It just looks so bad. The poverty, the crime. Ladera has more developed areas that have jobs and better conditions. But you know what I figured out?"

He glanced at her and pulled up an eyebrow.

"I think it's not all bad. There's some weird

security here that's less scary than the unknown. They know the rules. They have their friends and their families here. You know, maybe some of these people don't even know that there is anything better out there." She looked out the side window as she added, "And, of course, some, like your family, stay because they want to make it better."

He came to a red light and it was just fine because he needed to stop the car and just stare at her anyway.

She understood. Isabelle Rush, with her compassionate heart, had somehow managed to get to know him better in less than two weeks than his casual acquaintances in Miami had in years. Outside his family, Isabelle knew him better than anyone else. Or maybe she knew him better even than them. His family got only rare glimpses of the man he'd become in Miami while Isabelle saw him nearly every day.

And now, in the time they had spent together in Ladera, a bond had formed between them. She might struggle against it, but she could not deny it. And he was not giving up.

He wanted more of the way he felt when

he was with her, more of her smile, more of her sharp wit and dry humor, more of those maddening lips and the sound of her soft breathing next to him in the night.

He wanted her, all the way, forever. He wanted her as madly in love with him as he was falling for her. And he was going to do everything in his power to achieve that.

SONYA LAY ON HER SIDE on the recycled wood planks that made up the floor and listened to the people talking in the room below her, catching small shreds of conversation now and then, trying to tune out the noises that were coming in from the street. There were people out there, coming and going. She could hear women fighting, children playing games, men complaining about the government and the police. When she'd first been brought here, she had shouted her throat raw for help. Nobody outside paid her any attention.

She pressed her ear to the floor, wanting to catch as much as she could of the conversation that was deciding her fate. The men seemed to agree that to go back to the U.S. for the ransom money, after all that had transpired, was too risky. They were cursing someone named Fuentes and another guy who was apparently a doctor. Dr. Ramon, she thought they said.

Who were these men, and what did they have to do with her? Her head throbbed, making thinking nearly impossible.

The smell of smoke and food wafted in through the gaps in the wall, and she gagged. They had fed her earlier and she'd been too starved, wolfed down the meal too fast, ate too much. Now the food in her stomach was making her sick.

Voices rose below as the men argued. It seemed one or two got spooked and wanted to get rid of her in the river before they all got busted. The majority, however, were talking about a "buyer" for her. Some rich man to the east who would pay good money for someone he could use to fulfill his twisted pleasures. Not as much money as the ransom would have been if Fuentes and the doctor hadn't messed it up, but they were willing to take what they could get and cut their losses.

Then there was another argument about

whether or not she was in good enough shape for the man—if she could handle him for even a day, if he would be mad at them for bringing merchandise from which he couldn't get his money's worth.

Whoever he was, the men below didn't seem to want him upset.

One started yelling about the idiots who let her get this run-down, to the point where she was losing all value.

They seemed more nervous today than before, snapping and growling at each other like a pack of dogs. They wanted her gone, as soon as possible, as soon as they could agree on what to do with her.

She didn't have much time left.

She closed her eyes. Next time anyone came in, she would pretend she was near death—a fairly easy performance under the circumstances. She had to make them believe that she wouldn't survive the trip east, much less whatever the "buyer" had in mind for her.

Would they shoot her before tossing her into the river, or would they prefer to watch her drown? Either way, at least it would be over. She fought that thought.

Part of her, the rational side, wanted to curl up and give up. Her brain told her there could be no way out at this stage. Things had gone too far.

Yet another part, some stubborn corner of her heart, held on. It grabbed hold of the love she had for Juan, for her father, and wouldn't let go.

Did she have enough strength left to do anything? Even if she tried to escape, it was almost certain they would catch her, probably shoot her on the spot. Then again, wasn't that a fate preferable to becoming a sex slave to some sordid little man who might just torture her to death?

She lifted her hands to her face and began to chew at the rope, filled with a new resolution that gave her strength. The fibers were rough, scratching her gums and chapped lips until they drew blood. With her whole body aching, she barely registered the extra bit of pain.

Chapter Ten

"So where is Carrera?" Isabelle asked after Rafe thanked Enrique and clicked off the phone.

"In the slums of Maratiña. Word is, he messed up some major deal and he's lying low."

"You think Sonya is there with him?"

"Seems like a good enough place. The whole River Quarter is controlled by two rival gangs. They have a tacit understanding with police—the cops don't go in and they don't get shot by the rooftop snipers."

She swallowed. "Is it like Paco's shack city?"

Rafe looked over, with a *you wish* expression on his face. "Paco and his buddies are small-time. The River Quarter is...hard-core."

She resisted the urge to ask what *hard-core*

meant, exactly, in this context. No reason to get discouraged even before they got there. "How far are we?"

"About ten minutes," he said.

They'd been cruising the streets of Maratiña for the past half hour, waiting for Enrique's call.

"So how are we going to play this?"

"Friendly. Make sure your weapon is within reach for as long as they let us keep the guns."

"As long as they let us keep them?" She didn't like the way the conversation was going.

A few minutes passed before she spoke again. "Do we know exactly where Carrera is? I don't suppose Enrique gave a street address?"

"Hardly. We follow protocol and act very, very polite."

"Protocol?" she asked, then forgot the question at the view that opened before them as they turned a corner. "Is this it?" She examined the endless sea of shacks. "You got any friends in there?"

"Better," he said. "I know the boss."

"Well enough so he'll help?" She felt a nudge of hope.

He grinned. "Well enough so he'll give me

a minute or two for explanations before his men start shooting."

"Wonderful." She took in the hodgepodge of shelters made of corrugated cardboard, sheets of aluminum, rusty car hoods, driftwood, which leaned against each other. This wasn't a couple of empty lots taken over by the homeless and the criminally inclined. River Quarter was the size of a small town, its entrance surrounded by high-rise projects.

What she'd seen before was a shack village; this here was a shack metropolis.

Isabelle glanced up and wondered if the snipers Rafe had mentioned were on top of the roof. "Shouldn't we leave the car someplace safe?"

The guarded parking lot of an upscale restaurant they'd passed in the tourist district came to mind.

"If they let us in, we'll be okay. If they don't, it won't matter."

"Who are all these people?"

"A lot of them are immigrants from Bolivia and Paraguay. Others were displaced by various economic crises and were never able to get back on their feet."

"So they're not all criminals?"

He shook his head, his expression somber. "For the most they're just poor. The government doesn't have the resources or the interest to do anything about them. It's as if they don't exist. They have no power, the perfect environment for criminals. They come in, take over, exploit them and rule as they please."

Dozens of pairs of eyes followed their cautious progress, some hostile, some curious. Torn and still-dirty clothes hung on lines, naked and half-naked children ran around in groups, shouting, chasing each other. The car barely got past the first row of shacks before they were stopped by a team of teenagers, openly armed and looking rather menacing.

"Looks like security is here. Don't look nervous," he said.

Right. She drew in a deep breath, let it out, in and out again without being too obvious about it.

Three of the boys blocked the car while two walked up to the windows, one on Rafe's side, one on hers.

"I think you're lost, *amigo*. You wanna buy a map?" one of the boys asked in Spanish with a heavy local accent.

"I'm visiting," Rafe said.

The boy rolled his shoulders. "I think your visit just ended," he said as his buddies sneered.

"Is Jose Rey still around?" Rafe asked politely.

The teenagers looked at each other, then the one at Rafe's window said, "He was shot two years ago."

Rafe nodded. "I'm sad to hear it. We were friends when we were younger."

"What did you want with him?"

"Business."

The boy seemed to think on that for a while. "Sordado took over his business."

"His brother-in-law?"

"*Sí*. You know the man?"

He nodded. "We were in the riverfront riots together."

"No kidding?" The boy looked Rafe over, and so did the others, looking suitably impressed.

Riverfront riots? She'd have to remember to ask him about that later.

"Is he here?" Rafe was asking.

For a few moments, nobody said anything, each side measuring up the other. Then finally, the answer came. "*Sí*. Come with us."

Rafe got out and she followed him, leaving behind the safety of the car with some reluctance. The paved "street" gave way to a narrow dirt road a few yards in, wide enough only for the bike carts and wheelbarrows that used it for thoroughfare. An old man caned a chair in the shelter of an overhang, another was hammering a small piece of metal. She could smell food and see through the curtainless windows into crowded one-room adobes, where women cooked and took care of small children.

Passageways forked this way and that, the shacks laid out randomly as each occupant had chosen to build, following no pattern. Within seconds, she could no longer see the car. After a few minutes, she wasn't sure if she could find her way out of there again. She stuck close to Rafe.

The dizzying smells of unwashed bodies and human waste mixed with the aroma coming off large vats of frying meat. She watched people stand in line in front of a long shack, a foot or two higher than the others—some kind of community kitchen.

A string of lights were on inside, and she was surprised to see gas stoves under the vats.

"They have utilities here?" She glanced around and noticed, now that she was looking for it, wiring strung between shacks here and there.

"Pirated," Rafe said, and took her hand to draw her behind him.

The contact, his long fingers closing around hers felt reassuring.

They must have walked a good fifteen minutes before reaching their destination, something that looked very much like a lawn-mower shed moved here from a suburban backyard not long ago. It hadn't acquired the grime of the surrounding buildings just yet, its windows intact with glass.

The shed was set up on a much larger concrete foundation that must have supported a family home years ago before the River Quarter was razed and overtaken by the current inhabitants.

Three men sat around the entrance, two

of them in the dirt, one on a small stool. They pulled their weapons as the visitors approached.

"Qué pasa?" the one on the stool asked as he spit something brown near Rafe's shoes.

"Friends of Sordado," one of the teens responded.

The man looked Isabelle up and down then turned to Rafe. "Got a name?"

"Rafe Montoya."

The man paused a beat or two, then nodded. "Sordado says Montoya is dead."

And when she looked closer, she could see the small earpiece partially covered by his stringy hair. Sordado was somewhere nearby, listening in. Not in the shack, though—from there he could have easily communicated without electronics.

She glanced around at the surrounding buildings, her attention drawn back to Rafe as he was now rolling up his sleeve.

She relaxed her muscles, set her feet apart, getting ready for the fight.

But instead of lunging at the man in front of him, Rafe simply turned his upper arm toward the shed's door.

What the hell was he doing?

"Camera," he explained under his breath.

Still, it took her thirty seconds before she spotted the thing, cleverly attached to the doorjamb from inside, camouflaged by a dirty rag nailed to the doorframe.

"Take a look at your sorry-ass handiwork, *amigo*," Rafe said as he held his scar to the lens.

Another few seconds passed before the guard swung his rifle over his shoulder with a calculating look on his face. "Okay. Guns first, then in you go. Just the two of them." He jerked his head toward the teens with an expression that said "get lost."

Rafe handed over his weapon and so did she. The man patted them down with the efficiency of a true professional before opening the door for them, allowing entrance into the window-less, one-room shed that was lit by a bare bulb hanging from the middle of the ceiling. A pair of dilapidated couches hugged the walls. The man stepped in behind them, kicked one of the couches aside. It rolled on small black wheels to the middle of the room, revealing a staircase that led down.

"That way," he said.

Rafe went first, then Isabelle close behind him. She could hear the couch rolled back into place as soon as her head was under floor level.

"What is this place?" she asked in the complete darkness, reaching forward until she touched Rafe's back.

"Probably the basement of the house that once stood here," he said. "Here is the door."

The handle creaked as he turned it. "Here we are."

They stepped into the light of bare bulbs strung from the ceiling. The place was divided into several rooms and smelled like freshly ground coffee. She tried not to stare at the men who worked at long tables, nor at the brown packages they were working with. But she kept a tally of head-count and the guns she saw—about a dozen men, all well-armed.

Rafe headed straight to the back, where a handsome man in his forties sat in a worn leather armchair in front of a small desk, working on some documents, a series of stamps and inkpads in front of him and one of those lamps that were built into a large magnifying glass. A small copier hummed behind him.

He looked up and stopped what he was doing, stared at Rafe for a long moment. "Montoya." He nodded toward them. "I heard rumors."

"Sorry to hear about Jose. He was a good man," Rafe said, his tone friendly. "I'm glad to see you're doing well."

"I heard you got shot." The man watched him closely.

"Several times." Rafe flashed an easy grin. "They keep missing the important parts."

"I heard different stories, too." Sordado's voice turned colder. "That you crossed over to the other side. You here to make trouble?"

Isabelle forced herself to stay still and look not the least intimidated as tension crackled in the air.

The two men were about the same build and probably the same height, although it was hard to tell with Sordado sitting. In a one-on-one fight they would have been evenly matched. Of course, if it came to that, a fight between them would be anything but one-on-one. Sordado's men were all around them.

"I'm here to bring business."

"I'm not interested." Sordado flicked his wrist in a dismissing gesture.

"And to ask a favor from an old friend," Rafe added.

Another moment of tense silence passed.

"Who's the *chica?*" Sordado asked, shifting his attention to Isabelle. His gaze lingered over her considerably longer than necessary.

"She's my bodyguard," Rafe said, not quite succeeding at keeping his annoyance out of his voice.

But his words seemed to break the tension. A grin hovered over the other man's lips.

"I bet. Funny how you always end up with the prettiest woman around. I suppose some things never change. Remember Carmen?" He shook his head then. "Never mind," he said, and gestured toward a couple of chairs on the other side of his desk. "Sit and tell me about why you came back to put your life on the line after all these years. Maybe it'll help me decide what to do with you."

"CAN'T BE DONE." Sordado shook his head when Rafe was done with his proposal.

"You have enough people. Someone must know where Pedro Carrera and his men are."

The man shook his head again. "I know where they are. That's the trouble."

"We go in, get the woman out. It'll be done fast. You help us, you get the money." He had offered Sordado an even million dollars from the account Juan and Botero had set up for them for expenses. They hadn't been concerned about saving money, wanting nothing more than to get Sonya back.

"It's not about the money," the man said patiently, then added with a smile, "but of course, I'll take it. What I don't like is that Pedro and his men are in the back stands. It's Ricky Mentina's territory."

Rafe stilled at the name.

"Pedro would never work for Ricky." What game was Sordado playing?

"Not for him but under his protection. Times change." The man shrugged.

Ricky Mentina, Rafe turned the name over in his head and swore.

Ricky had been the man who'd tried to kill him at his niece's christening. Up until now, he'd been dealing with old friends and even they had been suspicious, ready to take him out if they decided he brought danger. Ricky would be another matter. He'd shoot first, ask questions later.

"If Ricky finds out I'm back, he'll hunt for me," he said, understanding well how that complicated things, why Sordado didn't want to get involved.

"I'd be willing to bet that promised million that he already knows. You had to talk to people to get this far."

"I didn't realize he was here."

"Seven or eight years now. He's a boss, you know."

Boss. Damn. That's all he needed. Ricky with real power. "Bigger than you?"

Sordado smiled. "Wants to be."

And the way he said that gave Rafe some hope. "So why not stop him now?"

"You know how bad the gang wars were for business. We have peace now. The Quarter exists in a delicate balance. Messing it up doesn't benefit anyone."

Rafe could certainly understand that. He leaned forward in his chair, examining the problem from every angle. Even if Sordado didn't help, it'd be helpful to have his tacit approval. At least they wouldn't have to worry about his people getting in the way.

"If I happen to do some damage to Ricky in the course of getting my work done, you wouldn't object?" He posed the question.

"I didn't say I wouldn't help at all," the man said, thoughtful, apparently finding the idea of inconveniencing Ricky more tempting than he'd let on. "Getting an exact location on this woman you seek shouldn't be too difficult. It's hard to keep secrets in the Quarter."

They were close. Almost there. Rafe glanced at Isabelle and could see from her face she was thinking the same. "I'd appreciate that," he said to Sordado.

"I might even be able to help you with Ricky a little. A small diversion. I can ask him to a meeting to discuss mutual business interests. He'll be suspicious." Sordado smiled. "He'll bring a lot of his men with him."

Which meant that Rafe and Isabelle would have an easier time moving around in Ricky's half of the Quarter. "Thank you."

"Where are you staying?" Sordado asked, and nodded when Rafe named their hotel.

"When do you think we'll be able to go in?" Isabelle asked.

Sordado looked her over appreciatively. "Tonight," he answered her with a charming smile then turned to Rafe. "On one condition."

"You'll get the money."

"I want something else as well. When you leave here tonight...I don't want you to ever return."

"You have my word on that."

"Good." Sordado nodded. "And now, forgive me, but I'm going to have to kick you out." He turned on his headset and spoke into the mouthpiece. "My visitors are done. Would you please escort them out? Make sure everyone understands they were not welcome here."

A minute later his goons were there to drag them up to the surface and shove them down the street amid a slew of threats and verbal abuse, giving a pretty convincing show for the onlookers.

THE MAN WHO CAME FOR THEM that night didn't introduce himself. He drove them in a black van to the River Quarter, then deep into it.

Isabelle gripped her gun as she watched the fires lit here and there in old steel barrels, the scary-looking men who gathered around them.

"You'll find your way out?" their guide asked as he stopped the van and shut off the motor.

"Yes," Rafe said.

"The people you are looking for are straight ahead. Look for the shed with no lights on and aluminum sheeting on top. You'll see it in the moonlight. The woman is up on the second floor." He slipped out of the van and disappeared into the darkness.

The dome light never came on. He'd probably turned it off to make sure they didn't draw attention to themselves when the doors were opened.

"Ready?" Rafe asked, his voice sure and full of strength, something she could hold on to in the darkness.

She took a deep breath and beat back her lingering fear and doubt. "Let's get her back." She slid out into the night and moved ahead, set on her course now.

Because Sordado's man had mentioned a

second floor, she had expected a real building, but their destination, about a hundred feet ahead, turned out to be nothing more than a two-story shack, the second floor built precariously above the first.

She stole up one side of the narrow alleyway and Rafe on the other.

"What do you want?" The challenge came from the shadows once they got within seven or eight feet of the door.

"Ricky sent a message," Rafe said, and stepped in the direction of the voice.

"Stop right there." The man, too, stepped forward, the barrel of his rifle glinting in the moonlight. "I don't know you."

"I just came in from the mountains." Rafe shrugged and pulled a piece of folded paper from his pocket that she recognized as some sort of advertisement they'd been handed in the hotel lobby earlier that day. "The message is for Pedro. You can pass it to him yourself if you want."

Isabelle stayed still, barely daring to breathe. The man hadn't spotted her yet, and she wanted to keep that advantage for as long as possible. She watched the door, the open windows, the black alleyways around them, ready to cover Rafe if necessary.

The guard was walking right up to him, reaching for the paper.

Rafe grabbed the rifle, yanking it forward while his other arm closed around the man's neck, squeezing until he went limp. He dragged the guy back into the shadows and laid him down quietly.

"Here, you take this," he whispered as he handed her the rifle when he came back. Out loud, he said, "*Gracias*. We'll be out in a minute." And walked through the door.

She slung the rifle over her shoulder and stepped in behind him.

Two men were watching a small black-and-white TV that stood in the corner.

"What is it?" one asked as he turned toward them.

She glanced at a makeshift ladder that disappeared into the ceiling. How many were there upstairs?

"I brought a message." Rafe's hand inched toward his gun.

She watched the men and backed toward the ladder. When Rafe started shooting down below, she didn't want to give anyone upstairs enough time to harm Sonya.

Without looking at her, Rafe seemed to know when she was in position.

"Ricky said to make sure—" He pulled his gun and squeezed off a series of shots, ducking behind the wooden crate when return fire came.

Isabelle flew up the stairs, threw herself to the right and rolled, narrowly avoiding the bullets that came her way. She took aim, clipped the man who was shooting at her, hit his shoulder. She was coming up when an arm shot out from behind her. The next thing she knew she was held immobile to someone's chest, her gun ripped from her hand with enough force to nearly take her finger with it.

"ISABELLE," RAFE CALLED OUT, not liking the sudden silence upstairs. "Isabelle?"

He took a last glance at the two bodies on the floor then stole to the bottom of the stairs without making a sound. He moved up, step by step, holding his gun ready.

Bullets came at him like possessed bees the second his head came up. He ducked down, swearing.

"Pedro, *hermano*. Pedro Carrera." He yelled the name, figuring his old friend had to be up there somewhere. "It's Rafe. I want to talk. Rafe Montoya, remember? We used to be like brothers."

A few shots were squeezed off in response, then came a voice he recognized as Pedro's. "Stop. Let him come up. If he's who he says he is, I want to see his face when I kill him."

He came up slowly, holding his pistol by the barrel, away from his body as a peace offering, desperate to get up there, to see what had happened to Isabelle.

Then he saw her and his blood ran cold. Pedro had her, his gun aimed at her temple.

A flash of surprise crossed the man's face, followed by so much hate it turned his cheeks red. He jerked his head toward Isabelle. "She anyone important to you?"

Rafe nodded, mapping the room, taking in the two other men and their weapons, the fact that he didn't see Sonya anywhere in sight.

"Good," Pedro said. "That should make this a lot more fun."

"Listen, I'm not here to cause trouble,"

Rafe said, keeping his voice calm and reasonable. "I'm here to take a problem off your hands."

"And what would that be?" Pedro sneered.

"Sonya Botero."

"She's dead," he said, but even as he did, a small scraping sound came from under the bed behind him.

He pretended not to hear and kept his attention on Pedro instead, noticing the way his eyes darted around the room, the needle holes in his arm, how the gun jerked in his hand every couple of seconds.

"You shouldn't have left," he said.

"You should have come with me." He'd asked at the time, but Pedro had refused.

"You betrayed everyone you knew." Rafe's one-time friend spat the words at him. "Things got worse. You don't know how bad it was for a while."

He believed that. Between the two of them, he'd been the stronger one. He had come to Pedro's aid countless times. It had to have been hard for him to be left to fend for himself.

"I'm sorry about that," Rafe said. "I had no choice. It was the only thing I could do."

Pedro swore at him, held the gun to Isabelle's head even tighter.

"You know how you said there was no point in going? That there was nothing outside of here?" Rafe slowly bent and placed his gun on the floor. If he were to find a way out of here for himself and the two women, it wasn't going to be through gunfire. "There are things, Pedro. A lot of things. You can turn your back on this place and walk just like I did. You can do it now. I will help. It'll be like old times, the two of us together, we'll make it work."

He caught a moment of hesitation in Pedro's eyes before his expression hardened again. "I'm not like you," he said, and there might have been a faint trace of regret in his voice. "For me, there's no way out."

"It's never too late." Rafe stepped forward.

And as Pedro grinned, he looked very much like the young man Rafe used to know, bringing a pang of regret to the mood of the room.

"You always were the optimistic one between the two of us," he said, his hand that held the gun relaxing a little.

He'll give in. But even as the thought

crossed Rafe's mind, shouting and gunfire came from outside.

Pedro turned to the window. "Ricky."

Apparently news of fighting in his territory had reached the man faster than they'd calculated. Rafe dove for his gun. A bullet came through the window just as his hand closed over the Beretta's handle. Pedro swore and let go of Isabelle, grabbed on to his chest, red seeping through his fingers. One of Ricky's men had inadvertently hit him from outside.

Rafe took out Pedro's men without hesitation, pulling Isabelle from the line of fire, pushing her to the floor next to the bed. Only he and his old friend remained standing now, their guns trained on each other, gazes locked.

Pedro breathed hard. More blood stained his shirt.

"Hermano." Rafe stepped forward. "Come with me."

He shook his head. "Go," he said and turned to the window. "I'll hold Ricky's men off."

He hesitated for a single second only, glanced back at Isabelle, who was helping Sonya from under the bed, pulling the rag from the bedraggled woman's mouth.

If he hadn't known who she was, he wouldn't have recognized her. In a sweaty, drab T-shirt and dusty jute sandals she looked nothing like the high society lady he'd met at a fancy reception. His newfound sympathy for Pedro weakened as he took in the woman's sunken eyes, her emaciated body. What the hell had those bastards done to her?

But there was no time to tear into Pedro now for the choices he'd made, the man he'd become. They had seconds to get away if they were to stay alive.

He bent and threw Sonya over his back then dashed down the stairs.

ISABELLE HAD A GOOD GRIP on the rifle, shooting at anything that moved.

Too late. Too late. The way out was blocked.

Rafe turned back, coming up again, shooting backward as he ran. She covered him, then when they were inside the room, she shoved the door closed behind them and the bed in front of it.

Pedro lay motionless a few feet from the window, his eyes glazed and staring into space.

Rafe's step faltered, but then he passed by

the man. "This way." He ripped off the curtain, tossed it out of the way and stepped up to the roof.

She could hear him talking to Sonya. "Hang on just a little longer. You'll be okay."

Isabelle swung the rifle over her shoulder and hustled after him.

"Montoya!" The shout overpowered the banging on the door behind them. "Face me, dog," someone shouted in Spanish.

The door splintered. Another few kicks and they'd be through it.

And, to her horror, Rafe stopped and turned back toward the room.

His face was so cold and hard, it sent a shiver down her back. This man who'd called for him, he knew. But he wasn't an old friend like Pedro. This man, he hated.

"Rafe!" She touched her hand to his. "Rafe?" She could hear the panic in her own voice.

For the first time since they'd arrived in Ladera, she saw Rafe's past reach for him to pull him back, and the moment was terrifying.

Then he looked at her and held her gaze for a moment before he turned and raced across the roof.

She scampered after him, covered him as people came around the corner of the shack and started shooting. More appeared in the window as Rafe switched Sonya from his shoulder to his arms and leaped for the roof of the next abode. They promptly crashed through it. Isabelle kept shooting as she followed his example, aiming for a spot that was still standing, trusting it to slow her fall.

The air got knocked out of her still. *Deep breath in, deep breath out. Keep squeezing the trigger.*

Where was he?

She turned and saw him elbow the outraged home owner out of the way as he ran through the back of the hut into a black alley. She didn't dare lag behind. She would never find her way out of this place on her own.

Men were running around in the dark, squeezing off shots randomly, rushing to the left, following each other's noise.

"This way," Rafe whispered once they were a few rows down. He zigzagged among the shacks, and just when she thought they were completely lost, he came out right behind the van.

She opened the back door and he laid Sonya in there. The woman seemed only semiconscious.

"Hang on. We'll be out of here soon," she heard him say as she rushed for the driver's seat and had the motor started by the time Rafe closed the back door and made his way to the front. She slammed on the gas, tearing through the piles of garbage that lined their path.

"Keep straight. Don't stop for anything. If anyone steps in your way, run him over." Rafe reached for the rifle she'd dropped between them and rolled down his window, leaned out to cover them from the gunfire that came from behind.

She dodged stray dogs and potholes that could have easily swallowed a front tire.

"What now? Which way?" she yelled when a burned-out car blocked their way.

"Left." Rafe kept shooting. "When you can make a right again, do it, then keep straight after that."

She did the best she could, the uneven road shaking the vehicle so much at this speed she felt like her kidneys would fall off before they got out.

But then she saw streetlights ahead and aimed for them, and a few minutes later they burst into the thin after-midnight traffic.

She drove as fast as the van could take it, ignoring red lights and one-way streets. They were almost at the other end of town before she dared to slow, her heart still pounding so hard she was surprised it hadn't beaten a hole in her chest yet. "Are we clear?" She glanced back at Sonya, then over at Rafe.

"You did it." He broke into a grin and tossed the gun aside, then took off his seat belt and crawled into the back, to Sonya. "You're safe now. We are going to take you to your father and Juan," he said to the woman, speaking so gently it made Isabelle fall in love with him all over again.

"I know you, don't I?" Sonya's question came on a rusty voice.

"I'm Rafe Montoya. We met a couple of times. Here, drink some water," he said.

"I thought you worked with Julia. What are you doing here?"

"Should we go straight to the airport?" Isabelle interrupted as she navigated the streets, and was stopped by flashing red lights at a railroad crossing.

"To the hotel first," Rafe said. "I'm sure Sonya would like to clean up. And we should, too. No need to draw attention." He pulled out his cell phone and made a call she couldn't hear thanks to the noise of the approaching train.

"Who was that?" she asked when the train passed and she stepped on the gas.

"U.S. embassy. They'll have a passport waiting for Sonya at the airport."

The next call was to Rachel to report that they had Sonya and everything was okay. Rafe looked rather smug when he hung up.

"What?" she asked.

"Rodrigo Santiago rolled over on Martinez. There *was* a political conspiracy, although Sonya's kidnapping wasn't part of it. Good to know the old instincts are still working," he said, all cocky.

"Yeah, you're a regular wonder."

He flashed a quick grin. "And don't you forget it."

"Thank you," Sonya said between two gulps, not putting the bottle down until it was empty. "What you two did…" She swallowed, apparently overcome by nerves and emotion. "It was a miracle."

"Wasn't as bad as it looked," Isabelle said, although wholeheartedly agreeing on the miracle part. She had trouble believing they'd made it and were all alive. But it was best for everyone involved if they played down the rescue. No need to blow their Weddings Your Way cover. "Actually, everything was carefully planned. Laderan law enforcement. Undercover," she lied through her teeth. "It would be better not to give a lot of details to anyone on this. Some of those men will stay in there. We don't want to jeopardize their lives."

She could see Sonya in the rearview mirror as she nodded solemnly. "Of course. I wouldn't want anyone to come to harm. I would like to… Could you find a way to thank them for me?"

"It'll be taken care of." Rafe finally figured out what she was trying to do and joined in.

Then they were at the hotel and Isabelle pulled in the back. She shut off the engine and flipped on the dome light, turned around to take a good look at Sonya at last.

"Are you okay?"

"Hard to believe it's over." She rubbed her wrists, which looked like they'd been chafed raw. "I wasn't sure— I tried to get away. It never worked."

"Come on." Rafe was opening the back door already and helping her out. "You're going to be fine now."

She nodded, tears beginning to roll down her face as she looked up at the hotel's marquee. "Are my father and Juan here?"

Isabelle exchanged a look with Rafe.

"They are still in Miami," she responded after a moment as she went ahead to open the door for them because Rafe was supporting Sonya. "They were very worried about you," she said, not saying more until they were in the elevator. Then, she didn't want to hold the news from Sonya any longer.

"Your father is okay now," she said. "But he had two strokes in the past couple of weeks."

"What? Oh, my God." Sonya collapsed against Rafe, the blood running out of her face. "Is he in the hospital?"

"He's at home. And he is recovering." Rafe scooped her up.

"I just— I thought you should know," Isabelle said, wishing now she'd waited awhile. But if it had been someone from her family, she would have wanted to know. "You can call him in a few minutes. And you'll see him tomorrow." The words felt good to say.

When they reached their floor, Rafe carried Sonya straight to their room, to the bed. "Here." He pushed the phone toward her with a smile. "Later, when you're rested, you can take a bath. I'll go and see if I can scare up some food."

Isabelle moved toward her backpack, which lay against the wall. "I have some clean clothes for you."

But she doubted Sonya heard her. She was already dialing.

Isabelle smiled and followed Rafe out of the room. "So who was that guy, calling after you? Ricky?"

"He and I go way back." He shrugged. "Last time I saw him, he tried to kill me, sprayed the church at my niece's christening. He swore if he ever saw me again he'd finish the job. I swore I'd kill him first if we ever met again. He is from another life. I have nothing to do with him now." He took a deep breath, looked back toward their room. "We shouldn't both leave her alone," he said.

"I'm not. I'll just guard her from out here for a while. I'm sure she wouldn't mind some privacy for her phone calls."

His masculine lips stretched into a smile as he stepped closer to her. "You're always thinking. You know, I like that about you. Among other things," he added.

God, he looked sexy disheveled like that, all heroic and fresh from the fight. "What other things?"

"Well, just as an example, I like the way you handle yourself in armed conflict. Terrifying really, but in a way also very sexy." He was just inches from her now.

She ignored the thumping of her heart. "And effective."

"That, too." He grinned agreeably and kissed her.

"I didn't think this was supposed to be part of the *just friends* thing," she said weakly when they pulled apart after some time, her body reeling.

His black eyebrows ran up his forehead.

"Never mind," she said and moved away.

He reached for her and pulled her back. "I want us to be friends."

"Sure. I—um, I should get back to Sonya."

But he wouldn't let her go. "Eduardo said—" He seemed flustered, which made her pause. "Anyhow, he said the reason why his and Juanita's marriage was so good was because they were best friends, too, not just lovers."

Her heart started into a slow, thumping rhythm.

"I think—" His hand on her arm softened into a caress. "I might not be any good at this, but I want to try. I want to try us, together. If you think you could stand a couple of dates with me. I've been thinking about buying a house and throwing some backyard barbecues. We could pick a place together and—"

The way he was looking at her just then, like she held his life in her hands, melted the last vestiges of resistance in her heart.

"Let's just start with a few dates and see where it goes from there," she said, happiness filling her as she stepped into the circle of his arms.

Chapter Eleven

"I love big weddings," Isabelle said as she looked at the bride and groom exchanging their vows, her gaze settling on Julia, a fellow agent and Sonya's best friend. She looked fantastic as maid of honor. She kept glancing at Luke, who sat in the back row and seemed to have eyes only for Julia. It was good to see the two so sappily in love. Another wedding to plan, Isabelle thought, and must have voiced the happy little sigh that hummed through her because Rafe looked at her and drew up an eyebrow.

Up front, Sonya gracefully slipped a diamond-studded wedding band on Juan's finger.

"I can't believe how much she's changed in two weeks," Isabelle said.

Sonya had filled out after her ordeal, her

bruises and scrapes healed. She had insisted on having the wedding on schedule, wouldn't hear of postponing, despite everyone telling her to rest for a few months. And maybe she was right. She certainly made a radiant bride.

It couldn't have been a more perfect day, with sunshine and a soft breeze off the bay, her father sitting in the first row with a beaming face. As stubborn as his daughter, he had insisted on giving her away although he'd had to walk down the aisle with a cane.

"I do," Juan said, his deep voice carrying all the way to the back rows. The look of pure love and adoration he gave his bride made Isabelle's eyes go misty.

She sniffed.

"Are you going to cry?" Rafe baited her.

"Of course not." She elbowed him. "It is a very touching moment, though."

"Mmm. I'm glad they made it here."

She stole a glance at Rafe.

Since they'd come back from Ladera, they'd fallen into some sort of relationship. They went out from time to time, had fabulous sex whenever possible, had long talks, went out on the bay and had more fabulous sex on his boat. It was all deceptively normal, except that she kept waiting for him to move on. She kept waiting to hear the words, "Look, it's been great while it lasted."

He'd been secretive lately, disappearing then changing the subject when she asked him where he'd been. There had been phone calls in which he would change the topic as soon as she walked in the room.

God, she hated how insecure she was becoming. It wasn't like her at all. But what she felt for Rafe scared her, because she recognized it as something a person was lucky to find once in a lifetime. He was it for her.

And the thought freaked her out so much, she'd been acting like an idiot lately—at times moody, at times trying to put some distance between them so her heart wouldn't break too badly if things didn't work out. She was taking this worse than any of her teenage crushes. She needed to snap out of it. They needed to talk.

The young priest gave the couple his blessing, ending the ceremony on a beautiful note.

Maybe that was her problem—being around

all these weddings and engagements, three just within the office in the last few months. Set a girl up for expectations of permanence. And, of course, Rafe Montoya never claimed to be a man who lived for commitment.

"I should go check out the Botero yacht one more time," he said next to her. "Want to come with me?"

"Sure." She hadn't had a chance to see the inside since it'd been decorated, having been too busy with last-minute PR duty.

He held out his arm and she took it as he glanced back one last time, probably to make sure that all security was in place. The wedding was secured to the nines. Apparently, he was satisfied because he turned back to her.

"Ricky is dead," he said casually, but she knew better.

"How? How do you know?"

"Eduardo called. A friend of a friend of a friend passed on a message."

She nodded, feeling oddly relieved. Rafe's news brought to mind another. "Did Rachel tell you about Maggie?"

"Haven't seen her since early afternoon. What news?"

"Señora DeLeon has been moved into the high security wing. From now on all her calls and visitors will be a lot more closely monitored. And her status had been updated to mandatory residency. Her family can't move her now even if they want to."

"That's what she needs," he said.

She smiled. "You're glad she's not going to jail, despite what she did."

"She didn't do it alone. She is disturbed. There was a lot of money involved. She could have been influenced—" He drew up an eyebrow at the amused look she gave him. "What? I'm not being chauvinistic."

"I know," she said. "I figured it out. You feel guilty because you were involved with drugs when you were young. I think you feel responsible for her."

He took a deep breath then nodded, and in the next second his serious look turned into a smile. "You know, one of the things I like about you is that you know me better than anyone else." His gaze held hers, then dipped lower, down the length of the silk gown she wore. "There is a Laderan poem about a young lover wanting to string the stars to drape them on the woman he loves. I don't think even a string of stars could make you look more beautiful than you are tonight," he said, and his easy charm shot straight to her heart.

She had got used to this, to the compliments, to the comfort of his company, to the instant heat his touch brought. "You're going to turn my head."

"That's the plan." His smile widened into a grin.

In another few steps they were at the dock. "So what do you think, she's not bad either, is she?" He was gesturing toward the Botero yacht.

On the outside, the vessel looked striking in Ladera's national colors, which were chosen not only to celebrate the wedding but to celebrate Juan's brilliant win at home, the majority of his bills passed into law.

They walked to the end of the dock, and only then did she see Weddings Your Way's own yacht behind Botero's, decorated just as splendidly in a shimmering pale green and white, obviously ready for some other event.

"Did we have anything else today?"

"Candlelit engagement on the water."

"Nobody tells me anything."

"It's a small, private affair. All they wanted was to rent the boat and have it stocked for the night. I'm sure once the wedding date is picked you'll be brought in for PR."

True enough. Rachel had no reason to bring her in at this stage. And she'd had her hands full with the DeLeon-Botero wedding.

She glanced back at the Botero yacht and spotted Sean Majors necking like mad with Sophie Brooks, another Miami Confidential agent, in the aft.

Apparently, Rafe saw them, too, because he gave a wolf whistle. "Get a room," he yelled up.

Sean called back a few suggestions on what Rafe could do with himself, but his voice lacked heat. The two men had put an end to their pissing contest and worked together at securing the wedding suspiciously like two friends would do.

"Might as well give them some time," Rafe groused. "Would you mind if I gave our boat a quick look-over first? The mechanic said the motor was catching this morning. He fixed it, but I want to check for signs of tampering."

He was thorough, and she liked that about

him. Weddings Your Way had been involved in a number of investigations over the years; some of the staff had made enemies. And although they could take care of themselves, Rafe took protecting them just as seriously as protecting their high-paying clients.

He hopped on first and held his hand out for her. "Welcome aboard."

His voice, rich and deep, skittered across her skin like a caress.

God, she was maudlin and fanciful tonight. Just because she was no longer on the clock, it didn't mean she shouldn't stay professional. "Can I help with anything?"

"You can check the cabins if you'd like. To make sure everything is set up right."

She nodded and went below, where lights had been left on for the couple that would be arriving soon. The CD player was going, too, she realized as she stepped inside and was surrounded by the soft sounds of a Spanish guitar.

The table caught her eye first, set with exquisite china, the best crystal, candles and a profusion of flowers. Champagne cooled in the ice bucket—Krug Champagne, 1990. Wow. She hadn't realized Weddings Your

Way even offered that. Who was getting engaged—she looked around with more curiosity now—the president's daughter?

The motor started, but she was too mesmerized by her surroundings to go up and see how Rafe was coming along. Then he ended up coming to her, appearing at the top of the steps.

"Everything looks okay, but I'd feel better if I took her for a quick spin," he said. "Unless you're in a hurry?"

"No. It's fine." The sumptuous elegance of the yacht was a wonderful place to be, even if for a few moments.

She could hear the anchor being pulled up and steadied herself as the boat swayed when Rafe steered it away from the dock. She meandered through the main cabin and opened the door to the larger of the two bedrooms, curious to see if any clues there betrayed the lucky couple's identity.

She found nothing but more champagne and more candles, the white silk bedspread nearly covered with deep-red rose petals—the whole setup insanely romantic. She backed out and went for the stairs. Maybe Rafe would know who rented the boat for tonight.

She came up from behind him as he stood at the wheel, his black tuxedo silhouetted against the setting sun.

"Everything okay down below?" he asked, over his shoulder.

"It's a dream."

"Good," he said, and cut the engine, then turned and looked her over, the fire in his eyes taking her breath away. He ran his hands down her arms, which the evening gown left bare. "Are you cold?" His voice caressed her.

She shook her head, unable to look away from his face as heat spread through her skin, starting from her wrists he kept loosely circled with his fingers.

He leaned closer and she lifted her lips, anticipating the kiss, but his mouth touched to her forehead instead, lingered there before moving onto one eyelid after the other. "I've never known anyone like you," he said, and lowered himself to one knee.

And then, finally then, the realization of what was going on hit her.

Her hands began to tremble, blood rushing to her head then out again, her brain just barely able to comprehend the scene.

The yacht was for them.

Rafe Montoya was proposing.

To her!

A hint of a smile hovered over his lips as he bent to her hands to brush a kiss over her knuckles before lifting his gaze again.

"Isabelle," he said solemnly, "I know this is kind of sudden, but hear me out. You know my past, you know the things I've done, things I'm not proud of." He took a deep breath and went on. "And I really hope you can live with that, because I don't think I can live without you. I um— Okay, I had this whole smooth speech planned, and I'm blanking big-time." He paused again. "The most important thing—I love you. What I'm trying to say is, will you be my wife? You know? Lover and best friend and all."

She blinked, stunned. "This is what you want?"

"More than my next breath," he said, and she'd never seen a man look more sincere.

"Yes!" She threw herself into his arms and he stood with her and spun her around, then just held her, held her close for a long time before he pulled away and kissed her.

Was that music filtering up from the cabin or were the stars singing above them?

"That was incredible," she said when they pulled away—just a fraction. "The yacht, the proposal, everything. Perfect. I didn't have a clue." She smiled.

"I was going to use my own boat, but I figured it'd tip you off. I wanted everything to be perfect. We've seen and heard stories of so many romantic proposals in this business." He grinned, keeping his arms around her. "I didn't want you to have anything less. I want to give you the best of everything."

"I have that, if I have you," she said, and then she kissed him.

* * * * *

Don't miss Dana Marton's next heartstopping romantic suspense with the release of UNDERCOVER SHEIK in January 2007, only from Harlequin Intrigue.

*Experience the anticipation, the thrill of the
chase and the sheer rush of falling in love!*

*Turn the page for a sneak preview of
a new book from Harlequin Romance
THE REBEL PRINCE
by Raye Morgan
On sale August 29th
wherever books are sold.*

"OH, NO!"

The reaction slipped out before Emma Valentine could stop it, for there stood the very man she most wanted to avoid seeing again.

He didn't look any happier to see her.

"Well, come on, get on board," he said gruffly. "I won't bite." One eyebrow rose. "Though I might nibble a little," he added, mostly to amuse himself.

But she wasn't paying any attention to what he was saying. She was staring at him, taking in the royal blue uniform he was wearing, with gold braid and glistening badges decorating the sleeves, epaulettes and an upright collar. Ribbons and medals covered the breast of the short, fitted jacket. A gold-encrusted sabre hung at his side. And suddenly it was clear to her who this man really was.

She gulped wordlessly. Reaching out, he took her elbow and pulled her aboard. The doors slid closed. And finally she found her tongue.

"You…you're the prince."

He nodded, barely glancing at her. "Yes. Of course."

She raised a hand and covered her mouth for a moment. "I should have known."

"Of course you should have. I don't know why you didn't." He punched the ground-floor button to get the elevator moving again, then turned to look down at her. "A relatively bright five-year-old child would have tumbled to the truth right away."

Her shock faded as her indignation at his tone asserted itself. He might be the prince, but he was still just as annoying as he had been earlier that day.

"A relatively bright five-year-old child without a bump on the head from a badly thrown water polo ball, maybe," she said defensively. She wasn't feeling woozy any longer and she wasn't about to let him bully her, no matter how royal he was. "I was unconscious half the time."

"And just clueless the other half, I guess," he said, looking bemused.

The arrogance of the man was really galling.

"I suppose you think your 'royalness' is so obvious it sort of shimmers around you for all to see?" she challenged. "Or better yet, oozes from your pores like...like sweat on a hot day?"

"Something like that," he acknowledged calmly. "Most people tumble to it pretty quickly. In fact, it's hard to hide even when I want to avoid dealing with it."

"Poor baby," she said, still resenting his manner. "I guess that works better with injured people who are half asleep." Looking at him, she felt a strange emotion she couldn't identify. It was as though she wanted to prove something to him, but she wasn't sure what. "And anyway, you know you did your best to fool me," she added.

His brows knit together as though he really didn't know what she was talking about. "I didn't do a thing."

"You told me your name was Monty."

"It is." He shrugged. "I have a lot of names. Some of them are too rude to be spoken to my face, I'm sure." He glanced at her sideways, his hand on the hilt of his sabre. "Perhaps you're contemplating one of those right now."

You bet I am.

That was what she would like to say. But it suddenly occurred to her that she was supposed to be working for this man. If she wanted to keep the job of coronation chef, maybe she'd better keep her opinions to herself. So she clamped her mouth shut, took a deep breath and looked away, trying hard to calm down.

The elevator ground to a halt and the doors slid open laboriously. She moved to step forward, hoping to make her escape, but his hand shot out again and caught her elbow.

"Wait a minute. *You're* a woman," he said, as though that thought had just presented itself to him.

"That's a rare ability for insight you have there, Your Highness," she snapped before she could stop herself. And then she winced. She was going to have to do better than that if she was going to keep this relationship on an even keel.

But he was ignoring her dig. Nodding, he stared at her with a speculative gleam in his golden eyes. "I've been looking for a woman, but you'll do."

She blanched, stiffening. "I'll do for what?"

He made a head gesture in a direction she knew was opposite of where she was going and his grip tightened on her elbow.

"Come with me," he said abruptly, making it an order.

She dug in her heels, thinking fast. She didn't much like orders. "Wait! I can't. I have to get to the kitchen."

"Not yet. I need you."

"You what?" Her breathless gasp of surprise was soft, but she knew he'd heard it.

"I need you," he said firmly. "Oh, don't look so shocked. I'm not planning to throw you into the hay and have my way with you. I need you for something a bit more mundane than that."

She felt color rushing into her cheeks and she silently begged it to stop. Here she was, formless and stodgy in her chef's whites. No makeup, no stiletto heels. Hardly the picture of the femmes fatales he was undoubtedly used to. The likelihood that he would have any carnal interest in her was remote at best. To have him think she was hysterically defending her virtue was humiliating.

"Well, what if I don't want to go with you?" she said in hopes of deflecting his attention from her blush.

"Too bad."

"What?"

Amusement sparkled in his eyes. He was certainly enjoying this. And that only made her more determined to resist him.

"I'm the prince, remember? And we're in the castle. My orders take precedence. It's that old pesky divine rights thing."

Her jaw jutted out. Despite her embarrassment, she couldn't let that pass.

"Over my free will? Never!"

Exasperation filled his face.

"Hey, call out the historians. Someone will write a book about you and your courageous principles." His eyes glittered sardonically. "But in the meantime, Emma Valentine, you're coming with me."

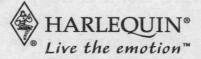

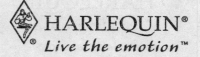

Harlequin Historicals®
Historical Romantic Adventure!

*From rugged lawmen and
valiant knights to defiant heiresses
and spirited frontierswomen,
Harlequin Historicals will
capture your imagination with
their dramatic scope, passion
and adventure.*

*Harlequin Historicals...
they're too good to miss!*

HARLEQUIN®
Presents

The world's bestselling romance series...
The series that brings you your favorite authors,
month after month:

Helen Bianchin...Emma Darcy
Lynne Graham...Penny Jordan
Miranda Lee...Sandra Marton
Anne Mather...Carole Mortimer
Susan Napier...Michelle Reid

and many more uniquely talented authors!

Wealthy, powerful, gorgeous men...
Women who have feelings just like your own...
The stories you love, set in exotic, glamorous locations..

HARLEQUIN®
Presents

Seduction and Passion Guaranteed!

SILHOUETTE *Romance*®

Escape to a place where a kiss is still a kiss...

Feel the breathless connection...

*Fall in love as though it were
the very first time...*

Experience the power of love!

Come to where favorite authors—such as

Diana Palmer, Stella Bagwell, Marie Ferrarella

*and many more—deliver modern fairy tale
romances and genuine emotion,
time after time after time....*

*Silhouette Romance—
from today to forever.*

Silhouette®
Live the possibilities